Breakin' Stones

Second Printing

Text set in Palatino
Copyright 1999 by Robert Holland
Printed on acid-free paper in Canada
ISBN 0965852350
Cover and title page illustrations by
Robert J. Benson

Frost Hollow Publishers,LLC
411 Barlow Cemetery Road
Woodstock, CT 06281
phone: 860-974-2081
fax: 860-974-0813
email:frosthollow@mindspring.com
website: frosthollowpub.com

I've had some help with this book and I thank my wife, Leslie, my daughter, Morgan, my son, Gardiner, and my brother, Bill, for their incisive comments and careful editing.

I also want to thank my old friend Jon Korper, the former editor of Soundings, for his invaluable assistance in helping me get the details right and for a final proofreading which proved beyond question what I've always known ... there is no better editor.

—R.H.

Breakin' Stones

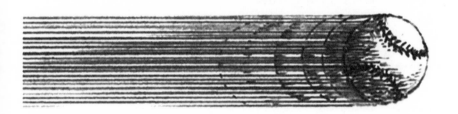

A novel of Sports and Mystery by
Robert Holland

FROST HOLLOW
PUBLISHERS, LLC
Woodstock, Connecticut

Robert Holland

Books for Boys

The Voice of the Tree
The Purple Car
Summer on Kidd's Creek
Footballs Never Bounce True
Breakin' Stones
Eben Stroud
Harry the Hook
Mad Max Murphy
The One-Legged Man Who Came Out of a Well
The Last Champion
Charlie Dollarhide
The Black Queen
Crossing The River
Stealing

For Younger Readers

Even Dogs Can Sing (poems and illustrations)

Other Novels

The Hunter
Conversations With a Man Long Dead
Things Got in the Way

Don't Ask

1

Rob English sat on the dry sand above where the seaweed marked the rise of last night's tide, watching the silvery water swirling round the bearded rocks the tide would soon cover again. Nothing, he thought, could rebalance things the way the tide did. By the clock it came and went, and it could be relied upon as few events beyond the rise and set of the sun.

The fish, of course, were less predictable. Sometimes they came in on the tide at just the spot you'd chosen. Other times they turned up off another beach, following schools of bait-fish or perhaps nothing more than a sudden whim, nosing up some likely current. What he found odd, because he had fished so many places on the Island at different times of day and different times of the year, was that he knew, as often as not, which beach to try. Still, that did not ensure catching fish. Today was a good example. He had chosen, on this Saturday morning in early March, to fish this particular Chilmark beach because he was certain no one else would fish here. After the nastiness of the past week, he just needed to be alone for awhile. Oh, there might be a walker or two, members of the Association that owned the beach, if only because the weather was so warm for early March with the temperature in the high fifties and the wind surprisingly still, but for the most part he would be alone.

The walkers might even stop to chat, and he wouldn't mind that, though he never seemed to have much to say to adults. How could you? How could you talk to anyone who kept asking, "what do you want to be when you grow up?"

Lately, it had gotten a lot more desperate. After all, he was a senior and in three months he was supposed to set out on a path that led somewhere. His folks assumed he'd join the family business as a carpenter, and eventually he and his older brother Carl would be partners in what was, by any measure, one of the best-run contracting businesses on the Vineyard. Only a fool would turn down such an offer.

Except that he wasn't at all like his brother. Not that Carl wasn't a good guy. Nobody could have wanted a better big brother, especially when it came to providing protection, because he was four years older and he'd always been one of those guys that no one tangled with. But they were not the same.

Rob, until last fall, when he had begun to grow, had been a dwarf. But he'd grown ten inches since then, and suddenly, at six-two, he was taller than all but a few basketball players, which was why his waders were eight inches too short. They were supposed to come up to his chest, but now they reached barely above his waist. And the feet were too small by a full size. He'd been leaving pages torn from Bean's and Cabela's around the house but so far his folks hadn't gotten the hint.

He stretched his legs. It was a lot to have grown in so short a time. He was now the second tallest in the family on either side. Only Grandpa Whitmore was taller, at six-four.

What it came down to was simply that he wasn't like other kids. And there were a lot of contradictions. He was thin, but he wasn't weak. He was smart, but he wasn't a good student. He was well-coordinated, but he played no sports. He wasn't the least bit shy, but could never think of what to say . He was also left-handed, and he had not even a glimmer about what he was going to do when he graduated from high school in June.

And worse, nobody let him forget about it. Tom was going to UMass, Charlie was headed for Colby up in Maine ... the list went on and on until it got to him. There was nothing after his name. It was old news. Five-foot-four-inch tall guys who carry pocket rocks in a high wind don't get much attention.

It would have helped to have had something at school that set him apart from other guys, but the two things he was good at didn't cut it. As far as he knew, he was the only kid on the island who fished with a fly rod, and he was the only guy he'd ever heard of who could knock one stone out of the air with another. These were clearly not the things girls noticed. He didn't even think they'd noticed how much he'd grown. Time after time he'd be talking to somebody and a girl ahead of them, recognizing his voice, would turn and look directly into his chest. And then she'd look up, puzzled and perplexed.

He looked down at his fly rod. An Orvis Trident, nine foot for eight-weight line, with an Odyssey reel. Six weeks of his last summer's pay driving nails for Dad. Carl thought he was nuts, even after he took him out for bass and he'd hooked into a thirty-five incher and let Carl play it in. Carl's view was that you went out to catch fish for meat. And on this island with a fisherman behind nearly every mailbox, that was normal.

Usually he kept some fish to eat and some to smoke, and let the rest go. What he liked most was getting them to rise to his fly. He liked knowing that he could look at a patch of water and know where a fish might lie, even when the gulls and terns gave no indication that fish were feeding. It was one mystery he could solve, and since his whole life seemed to be a mystery that defied solution, it was nice to have one he could master.

Rob stood and looked out over the water. It was a good day for fishing, the sky gray, the water running silvery, and the fish would not be so shy and ... what was that?

His eyes followed a plank drifting on the tide. It looked like plank from a boat hull, and on the end where it had been broken, the splintered wood was light in color, meaning it had not been in the water very long. He watched it float slowly by, appearing and disappearing among the rocks as it drifted along the beach and off toward the next point.

He set his rod on a large flat rock and walked down to where the sand was hard underfoot, bent and picked up several stones the right size for throwing. It would be a half hour before the water would have come in far enough to fish, so it wasn't like he'd risk scaring anything off. It was a way to pass time, something he'd done since he could remember. Throwing stones.

He looked at the plank floating past some seventy feet away, wound up like a big league pitcher and fired the stone. It hit the plank dead center and then he threw another four stones, hitting the plank each time. But he didn't just hit the plank, he hit it so hard with the last stone that he split it in half.

The force of it surprised him. He knew he could hit it, but he had not known that he could throw so hard. He grinned. Whoa. Was this the result of growing taller? Must be. What else could explain it?

Next trick. His best. He threw one stone high into the air, and then he fired the second stone to intercept the first as it fell earthward. No contest. He'd been doing this for years.

He tossed the first stone in a long, steep arc and then fired the second stone. They intercepted perfectly but the collision shattered both stones. It looked like a clay bird when you got the shotgun on it just right. It was awesome! Totally awesome! He picked up two more stones, fired the first one out over the water and then, timing it carefully, he threw the second stone. The result was the same. Just wait till the summer kids showed up with their money this year. For years he and Carl had been hustling the summer crowd, sometimes making forty or fifty bucks a night. But now, after they got them the first time, they could double the bet on whether he could break the first stone.

He tried it again, and again he shattered the dropping stone. Then he cut down the speed and just knocked the first stone from the air.

The voice took him by surprise.

"That is one hell of a trick," the man said.

Rob turned.

"If I hadn't seen you do that, I wouldn't believe it could be done. And yet I've just seen you do that four times in a row. How on earth did you learn how to do that?"

Rob grinned, looking at the man carefully. He was in his sixties, he thought, wearing chinos, a blue windbreaker, and a baseball cap with a logo he'd never seen before. "I just tried it and then I kept doing it."

The man stepped closer and stuck out his hand. "I'm Hal Farrow," he said.

Rob shook hands. "Hi, Rob English." Now, as he looked more carefully, he could see that the man was probably younger than he had looked at first because now he could see that the lines in his face had come from being outside and not from age. He was a shade under six feet tall and he looked trim and fit. Moreover, he had a hand like a clam basket, it was so big.

"Could you do that again?"

"Sure." Rob picked up two stones and repeated the trick.

"How come it breaks sometimes?"

"I throw the second stone harder," Rob said.

"That's even more incredible." He shook his head in disbelief. "Do you live here in the Association?"

"No," Rob said. "On Middle Road."

"Oh," the man grinned. "A real Islander."

Rob nodded.

"And a fly fisherman."

Again Rob nodded.

"Pretty darn good equipment too."

"I was at the Orvis contest last June and one of the men from the company let me try out a Trident."

"Did you win?"

Rob shook his head. "Came in third."

"Pretty respectable finish with a whole beach full of experts." One surprise after another, first the stones, and then his handshake with a grip like a bolt cutter, and then, of course his ability with a fly rod.

"A school came through but I wasn't strong enough to get my line out to them. I was kind of short then." He grinned. "This year it'll be different."

Hal nodded. "Somehow I expect it will." He gestured toward the water. "Do you fish here often?"

"Once, maybe twice a year."

"I don't think I've ever seen anyone fishing here."

"Are you here year-round?"

"As of today," he said. "I retired on Monday and we packed up everything and left. Now we're here for good."

Rob grinned. "I can't imagine a better place to live."

Harold's eyebrows arched upward. "You're a senior?"

"Yes, sir."

"No. Call me Hal. You're close enough to being a man to start calling men by their first names, I should think." He took off his cap, smoothed his gray hair, and reset the cap. "You must be a pretty good ballplayer."

"I've never played since Little League."

"Really? Now how is it a young man who can throw like that isn't playing baseball?"

"I'm going through a big growth spurt," Rob said. "I've grown ten inches since last fall. When I was five-four, I couldn't do much in the way of sports."

"Not even soccer?"

"Too slow."

"Wait a minute. Your last name is English? You live on Middle Road?"

Rob nodded.

"Your dad and brother built our house for us."

"I worked on it this past week. We went 'til ten every night to get it ready. It's a very nice house."

"And your dad and brother are the best builders I've ever seen. Are you going to join them when you graduate?"

"I don't think so," Rob said.

"You're going to college then?"

"No. I'm not much of a student. I read a lot, but I just don't apply myself, or at least that's what I keep hearing from my teachers. School's kind of boring."

Hal looked out at the water. "Tide's almost right, I'd say."

Rob looked around at the water which was now about half-way up the rocks, figuring that if Hal knew that, then he had to be a fisherman.

"Well, I'm going for a walk. Good luck," he said, and then turned away toward the east.

"Thanks," Rob said, "It was nice talking to you."

"Pleasure was all mine, Rob."

He watched Hal walk off down the beach and then walked up and got his rod, irritated by Hal's assumption that he must be going to college. Heck, not everybody went to college, especially not here. So what was the big deal with not going to college? What had irritated him, he thought, was having the subject rear its nasty, ugly head again.

He waded out into the chill water, unhooking the fly from the keeper just above the grip on the rod, then working the rod back and forth to get some line out. He was almost waist deep when he stopped and began to cast. And now his casting was different too. Now when he shot his arm forward in the forecast the line exploded through the guides, reaching out and out and dropping the fly farther than he had ever cast before.

He was tempted to haul in and cast again, just because he could do it, but he controlled the urge. The water was too still for that, and any extra thrashing would only spook the fish ... if there were any fish there. No. It would spook them because there were fish here. He could feel them in a way that he had never been able to explain. He just knew when fish were near.

But they were deep now, working around the rocks in search of the bait fish that came in on the tide, so he let the line sink, guessing the distance to the bottom before beginning his retrieve, making the fly dart about like a shiner being chased.

Cast after cast he concentrated on trying to get the fly to drift toward the base of one enormous rock, but the current was running strong, and the fly swept through too quickly. He changed his angle, walking to the right nearly twenty feet. Last year he couldn't have made this cast. It was at least ninety feet.

He stripped out line and began working the rod. It was incredibly powerful, but it was still a long, long reach. And it was more difficult because he was standing deep in the water, meaning his backcast was much more likely to hit something behind him. The trick was to carry seventy feet of line in the air and then have enough free line in the stripping basket belted around his waist, so on his final cast forward the weight of the line and the combined thrust of the rod and his arm would pick up the loose line and shoot it out through the guides on the rod to pick up all the slack line and lay it out on the water.

It was, like anything athletic, a matter of power and timing, because no matter how strong you are, if you don't make the final push at the right instant, there is no power available. He could feel the line in the air, sensing how it swept out behind him in a nice tight curl, and then he put it together and the line hammered out through the guides right down to the reel. Damn, he was good!

The line sank quickly and this time it was in the right place, the fly working deep, right along the base of the rock to where the current eddied. It was a place a fish might wait and ... the force of the strike pulled the rod downward, the tip flexing fully before the butt section of the rod began to bend. The reel screamed savagely as the fish ran for deeper water. Rob tightened down the drag, holding the rod up high so the fish had to work against the full flex of the rod and the drag on the reel.

It slowed and turned and he took back some line, getting almost all of the backing in before the fish turned for another run. Rob snubbed that run off as well, and then just as he was ready to relax, the fish wheeled and came at him. Now there was no time to reel and he simply stripped in line as fast as he could, keeping enough tension on the fly so that the fish couldn't shake it loose. A lesser fisherman would have lost the battle there, but Rob had been ready, and the instant the fish hit shallow water it turned, and all he had to do was let out line until the fish slowed as it worked against the weight of the line.

It was a big fish. Maybe thirty pounds, but he could feel the lack of vitality that so often occurred in the bigger fish. Which meant, he thought, that it was probably a spent cow, a female that had already spawned up in a river somewhere and hadn't yet got its strength back.

Slowly the runs grew shorter, and finally he began to back toward the beach. Now the fish just followed and he led it in. The fight was gone. He reached down, picked the fish up by the gill, and dragged it up onto the beach. It was at least thirty pounds. He slipped out his long fish knife and stuck the fish down through the back of the head, killing it instantly.

This was a money fish and it meant he was going to quit and take it into Menemsha and see how much either Poole's or Larson's would pay. It was early enough in the season, so he knew he'd get a good price. There were very few bass around.

He unhooked the fly, slipped it into the keeper, set the rod on a rock, and walked to the water to wash the slime from his hands. When he looked up, the water was full of planks. They must have been just beyond the point. It was, he thought, a substantial mystery. Somewhere a boat must have blown up, and it hadn't happened very long ago, judging by the freshness of the paint and the light color of the broken ends of the boards.

He watched a big chunk drifting in and he waded out, grabbed hold, and pulled it into shallow water. The white paint had been badly scorched, and it sure did look like a boat had gone up somewhere. But that wasn't uncommon. Every season some idiot started his boat without venting the engine compartment of gas fumes. Yet something was wrong with that idea, he thought as he looked down at the piece of hull in front of him, he just couldn't think what.

He knew he was going to have to figure it out, no matter how long it took. It wasn't even a matter of having to solve the mystery, so much as the need he felt to pry into things. He grinned to himself. It was a good thing he wasn't a cat because if he were, then his mother would have been right, and he'd have been dead. On the other hand, he thought, it wasn't really curiosity that killed the cat. He'd watched a lot of cats. What got them in trouble was that they got so focused on what they were poking their noses into that they could not react to trouble from another direction. When you grow up as the runt of the litter, survival depends on being prepared.

It was why he heard the foot steps in the sand long before the man who was making them had closed to within fifty feet.

Time And Tide 2

"What'd you find?" Hal asked as he walked toward him over the hard sand.

Rob grinned. "One big bass," he said, pointing to the big fish lying on the sand. Like like all stripers it was a fine looking fish, silvery and greenish blue, with dotted stripes running down its sides.

Hal stopped, looked down at the fish, and laughed. "And everyone I asked said there was no point in fishing for stripers until April, at the earliest. That is a great catch, Rob."

"Thanks."

Hal stood with his hands in his pockets. "Do you always kill your fish?"

It was a question he didn't like, but because he fished so often among other fly fishermen, who usually threw their fish back, it was one he'd heard before. "I've got a commercial license," Rob said.

"Sorry about that," Hal said, "it was a stupid question."

"I keep enough to eat and some to sell," Rob said.

Hal smiled. "Guess I've forgotten how hard money is to

come by when you're in school." He pulled his hands from his trousers and lodged them in his jacket. He laughed softly. "Fishing is a noble way to make money."

Rob smiled. This guy was okay. "Sorry if I was a little grumpy," he said. "I get tired of questions sometimes."

Hal's eyebrows arched as he thought about the surprising young man in front of him. "Why did you decide to fish here?"

"I thought there might be fish here."

"Nothing else?"

"Nobody around, usually." He looked up at the 'P' insignia on Hal's cap. "What team is that?"

"Team?"

"Your hat."

"Oh, the Pittsfield Mets. It's a Class A team."

"Did you come from there?"

"No. Connecticut." He pointed to the piece of boat hull bobbing gently in the water. "What do you make of that?"

Rob scratched his head. "It's a piece of a boat hull."

"I found another piece down the beach."

"It's a little weird," Rob said. "It was a big boat, maybe forty feet, but I haven't heard about a boat blowing up."

"Probably some perfectly logical explanation."

"I suppose."

"But you don't think so."

Rob pointed to an area where the paint on the outside of the boards had been blistered black. "When most boats blow up, it's because somebody forgets to vent the engine compartment, but it looks to me like this boat blew up from the outside. And it went down fast, before the wood had a chance to catch fire." He pointed to the edge of the blackened area. "It must have blown the bottom out of it."

"How do you know how big it was?"

"Because of the curve in the hull. I mean, it's just a guess, but I've helped my grandfathers build a couple of boats."

"Sounds like a pretty good mystery," Hal said. "Even so, I'd bet it can be explained easily enough."

Rob nodded. "I just can't think how," he said. "There's probably a perfectly plausible explanation." He put his foot against the section of hull and pushed it back into deeper water, turned, and picked up his fish. "Gotta get this over to Menemsha," he said, "while it's nice and fresh."

"Should we notify anyone?"

"I'll tell the Coast Guard," Rob said.

Together they walked up the beach and onto the soft sand path back to the small parking area, Rob lugging the fish easily, and not really thinking much about it until they reached his battered canvas-topped Jeep. Clearly, he was not only getting taller, he was getting stronger.

Hal stopped as Rob laid the fish on the back floor, clipped the fly from his line, and began putting his gear away.

"Aren't you afraid you'll get towed without a sticker?"

"Off season the beaches belong to everyone."

"Some pretty crotchety people in this association," Hal said.

"They could call, but the tow truck wouldn't come. And if it did, they'd see it was my Jeep, and they'd leave and bill the Association for their time."

"But in the summer they'd tow you."

"Sure. They can charge whatever they want then. But the only Islanders parked here then are real estate agents."

Rob hung his waders in the back of the Jeep, put on his New Balance cross trainers, and closed the back . He reached out and offered his hand again. "It was nice to have met you. If you want to go fishing sometime, give me a call."

"You're sure about that."

"I'm sure."

"Well, I'll do that, then."

Rob climbed into the Jeep, started it, shifted into first and pulled away. As he came around the small circle, he waved, and then headed out the long sand and gravel track to the North Road. Not until he stopped at the end of the road to check for traffic did he understand what had just happened. He'd actually carryied on a conversation with an adult! How the heck had that happened? Maybe you really do grow up, he thought.

The run to Menemsha took only a few minutes, and a few minutes later he'd sold the fish to Larson's, and headed for home. Usually, he'd have tuned to a rock station on FM, but this time he tuned in a local station looking for news about a missing boat. Nothing.

He pulled into the Chilmark post office to pick up the mail and as he came out, Tommy Kincaid pulled in next to the Jeep in his old Volkswagen convertible. He sat slouched down in the seat which was now the cool way to drive, looking like you were a dwarf. Not only was Rob through with being a dwarf, but his legs were now way too long to allow him to slouch in the cramped Jeep.

"Hey," Tommy called. "S'up?"

He set the mail on the passenger seat and walked over to Tommy's car. "Not much. How about you?"

"I am like totally bored, man. I mean, here it is like Saturday morning and there is nothing to do!"

"You need a project, Tom," Rob said.

"Sure. Like work, right? Hey, man, I work all summer. Now it's time to hang out. Time to play!"

Rob looked down at his watch. It was only nine o'clock. "Aren't you up kind of early? I thought you usually slept 'til noon on Saturday."

"Baseball tryouts. I got up early so I'd be ready."

"What time do they start?"

"Noon." Tom looked closely at his oldest friend. He recognized the look, a kind of curious glint in his eyes, a certain way his mouth turned up at the corners. "Don't tell me you're thinking of trying out?"

"I'd like to have tried out for one sport before I graduate." He laughed. "Hey, nothing ventured, nothing gained, right?"

Tom didn't know what to think. Mostly he didn't want Rob to end up looking like an idiot, and not just because it might make him look bad. "We got some pretty good players," he said. "And I gotta tell you, Robbo, trying out for the first time as a senior, you've got about zero chance."

"You sound as if you don't want me to try out."

"It isn't that, Rob, it's just that, well, listen. When was the last time you played ball? Fifth grade?"

"Yeah, I guess so."

"These guys have been playing ball every spring and summer. They're always in a league somewhere."

"Still, it can't hurt to try out."

"Have you even got a glove?"

"Sure. Follow me to the house. We'll get some coffee and throw the ball a little. Loosen up."

"Hey man, it's your funeral."

About a mile and a half down Middle Road they turned onto the long dirt driveway that wound its way back into the woods, climbing steadily until they broke out into an open field.

The house, with its nineteen twenties cottage-style architecture, seemed to have grown up out of the hill. It looked low and close to the ground, but that was only the illusion created by the sweeping roof lines shot through with gables, and the broad porch that cut across the front of the house.

They parked in the circular drive.

"It may take me a second to find my glove," Rob said.

"See? I knew you weren't up to this."

As it turned out he couldn't find his glove and he grabbed Carl's from the shelf in his room. Not many families had two left handed kids.

"How about spikes?" Tom asked. He looked down at Rob's feet. "You've got some huge feet, there, Robbo...."

"I'll have to buy spikes, I guess." Rob grinned as he opened the glove and found a ball inside.

They went back outside and Tom fished his catcher's mitt from the trunk of his car. Then they stood about thirty feet apart on the broad flat lawn and began tossing the ball back and forth. As anyone who has ever done that can tell you, nothing seems to promote conversation like having a catch. Tom watched carefully, looking for any lack of coordination, but Rob caught and threw the ball as if he had been doing it all his life.

"So," Tom said, "Who you taking to the prom?"

"Nobody." Rob wrapped his fingers around the ball and tossed it back. It felt big and almost clumsy compared to the beach stones.

"You're not going?"

"I never have so far. I thought I'd keep a perfect record."

"Yeah, but you were a midget then. Now you're one of the tallest guys in school."

Rob caught the ball, backhanding it, and then he threw it back, a little harder this time. He might not have played but he'd spent a lot of time watching the Red Sox. And now, as he threw the ball, he realized that he had spent an unusual amount of time watching the pitchers, even though he had not been aware of it. "I may be taller, but I don't think anyone has noticed."

"I wouldn't bet on it," Tom said.

"I don't pay much attention to that stuff," Rob said. "Force of habit, I guess."

"Just what position are you going to try out for?"

"Pitcher."

"Whoa! Talk about cojones. The guy never plays and he wants to try out for the toughest position on the team. Worse, we like, already got three good pitchers."

Rob grinned. "Process of elimination. I don't know whether I can hit, I'm too slow for the outfield, and I'm probably pretty shaky on ground balls, but I can throw, Tommy boy, I can throw."

"Well let's see what you got then." He walked over to Rob, dropped a stick in the grass, and then turned and paced off sixty feet. "Okay, that's the right distance." He squatted down and held up his glove as a target. "You ready?"

Rob set his left foot next to the twig and rocked back into a full windup, his right leg rising very high, his body tight and compact, and then he stepped forward with his right foot, pushing hard with his left as he drove his body toward Tom, and let the ball fly out of his hand.

The ball didn't even look like a ball in the air. It was a white blur above the grass, and it rose coming in, 'til it was belt high when it smacked into Tom's glove.

"OW!" Tom leaped up, throwing his glove and the ball to the ground and rubbing the palm of his hand, but aware, even through the pain, that a guy he had known all his life, a guy who had been a midget, a guy whose only talent had been catching fish, had suddenly shown a talent that was enormous, by any measure. "Damn that hurt!" He picked up the glove and ball and tossed the ball back to Rob as he worked his hand into his glove. "When did you learn to do that?"

"I told you I could throw."

"Throw is one thing, Robbo. That was pure smoke. And it was a strike too." He walked toward his car.

"You quitting?"

"No. Just getting my sponge. You throw too hard." He picked the sponge out of his gear bag, slid it into the glove, and squatted back into position. It had to have been an accident. "Okay, give me another one." He held the target to the left, figuring to catch the ball in the web of the glove. But it was too fast. Rob aimed at the center of the glove and hit it before Tom could slip it to the side to avoid the full force of the ball. If anything it was faster and the smack seemed as loud as a rifle shot.

Tom threw the ball back to him without standing up. The sponge helped, but it still hurt. Damn he threw hard! None of their pitchers threw anywhere near this hard.

Carl stepped out onto the front porch. He was just under

six feet tall, blond and blue-eyed like his younger brother, but he had thick arms, and he was broad through the shoulders. He walked to the edge of the steps and stood, leaning against one of the white columns. "What was that noise?" he asked.

"It was the sound of someone getting his hand mangled," Tom said.

"By what?" Carl asked.

"By your brother the ex-midget."

"Rob?" He looked incredulously at his brother. "What'd he use, a rifle?"

"I wish he had. It wouldn't hurt as much."

Carl jogged down off the steps. "This I gotta see," he said. "Let me borrow your glove, Tom."

"Sure." Tom handed him the mitt. "Keep the sponge in, Carl. You're gonna need it."

He slipped on the glove, positioning the sponge just behind the pocket, and squatted down.

"Okay, pitcher, fire it in here," Carl called.

The result was the same, except that this time it was Carl rubbing his hand and glowering back at his brother. "Where in hell did you learn to throw like that?"

"I got bigger," Rob said.

"Not that big..."

"I didn't know he could throw at all," Tom said.

"Oh, he can throw for accuracy. He can even throw one stone in the air and hit it with a second stone." He grinned.

"We've made more than a few bucks on that, right Rob?"

Rob nodded. It was hard to keep from smiling when your older brother offered up the praise.

"Okay," Carl said. "You guys wait here. I'm gonna get another piece of sponge and check this out a little more."

Tom walked over to his friend. "Okay, question. Can you throw a curve or a slider?"

"Nope. But I know how to hold the ball and I've watched guys throw those pitches. I could do it."

Tom stood silently for a second or two, just staring up at his oldest friend. Then he burst out laughing. "Damn! Damn! Damn! I never saw a pitcher last year who could throw that hard, and nobody on our team can even come close. That last one had to be close to ninety miles an hour!" He poked a finger into Rob's chest. "And another thing. I wanna see this trick with the rocks. And I wanna know how come you never told me anything about any of this."

Rob shrugged. "It's just a trick. Lots of people can do tricks."

"Not stuff like that, they don't. C'mon, show me."

They walked over to the gravel drive and Rob picked up a couple of suitable stones. He tossed the larger of the two into the air and then nailed it coming down with the second stone, both stones shattering in the air.

"Whoa! You didn't just hit it, you busted it! I gotta tell you, man. That is like very, very intense. I never heard of anyone who could do that!"

"It's no big deal, Tom. I probably threw about five million stones before I got it down. You practice anything enough, you're bound to get good at it."

"Yeah, some things, but this is just not one of those things."

Carl came back out with a thick piece of sponge and stuffed it into Tom's glove along with the first piece. George English followed him out. "Okay," Carl said. "I brought an ump this time."

They paced off the distance a second time and Carl squatted down, George standing behind him. "You're not gonna believe this, Dad," he said as Rob began his wind up.

The ball seemed to explode out of his hand and then a millisecond later it smacked into Carl's glove. It hurt even through the sponges, but he wasn't about to tell him that. There was such a thing, after all, as too much praise.

Ten pitches later he stopped and stood up. "That's enough for now," Carl said. "How's your arm feel?"

"It's fine," Rob said. He walked over to where they stood, taking considerable satisfaction from the fact that while his father might not have been shocked speechless, he sure wasn't saying much.

"I told you, Dad," Carl said. "Even that summer I played in the Cape Cod League no one threw that fast."

George English shook his head, then ran his right hand back over his dark blond hair, before shaking his head again. "I don't even know what to say."

"The word agent comes to mind," Carl said.

"What?" Rob laughed. "I haven't even made the high school team yet!"

"What do you think, Tom?" Mr. English asked.

"It'll take Coach two batters to make up his mind, and then Rob'll be pitching the season opener. He just throws the ball. He doesn't aim, and he throws with his legs the way you're supposed to." He looked around at Rob. "All we gotta do is find a college for you. It's kinda late, but after you pitch a couple of games there's gonna be scouts all over the place."

"I'm not much interested in college," Rob said.

"Hey," Carl said, "this is baseball we're talking here. This is the sport that has its own farm system."

"Now just slow down here," George English said. "There's plenty of time, and unless things have changed since I played ball, in this game you do things one game at a time." He looked up at his son, seeing him differently than he ever had before. "What do you know about the game?"

"I've watched a lot of baseball, Dad," Rob said.

His father nodded. "But that's not enough. You've got a lot to learn in a very short time." He clapped him on the left shoulder. "You up to that?"

"Sure." He grinned. "As long as I don't have to write some dumb paper on it."

"No, no papers. Just baseball, baseball, and more baseball."

And suddenly he could see the logo on Hal's hat, and that reminded him that he hadn't told them about the fish. "I caught a thirty-pound bass this morning."

"Thirty pounds? Where?" his father asked.

"Spring Point."

"I wonder if Mr. Farrow and his wife moved in on schedule. I ought to call."

"They did," he said. "I met him on the beach. Seems like a nice guy."

His father looked suddenly worried. "I better call and see if everything's okay." That attitude was part of why he did so well as a contractor. He always made sure he'd done the job right, and he always made sure the customer was satisfied.

"Hey, that reminds me," Rob said. "Did any of you hear about a boat blowing up somewhere?"

"Like when?" Tom asked.

Rob shrugged. "Last couple of days, a week at the most. There was a lot of stuff in the water at Spring Point, planks and even a four by six-foot section of hull. The broken ends were fresh."

"Did you talk to the Coast Guard?" Carl asked.

"Maybe I oughta run over there." He turned to Tom. "You wanna take a ride?"

"Sure."

"While you're gone, Carl and I will work up a training schedule."

Rob frowned. "A schedule?"

His father nodded. "You have to learn how to take care of

your arm, how many pitches to throw at any one time, how to keep the muscles loose so you don't tear something."

"I hate schedules, Dad."

Carl laughed. "Get used to 'em," he said. "You've got what they call a live arm, Robby. But you have to be real careful or you'll use it up."

"Pretty complicated."

Carl shook his head. "Just common sense, little brother. Just common sense. And you're going to have to learn some strategy and how to throw a change-up."

"What about a curve?" Rob asked.

"First we make sure your arm is strong enough to take the punishment," his father said. "You've grown a whole lot, real fast, and we have to make sure the muscles have caught up."

"Listen to what your dad's saying, Rob," Tom said.

"Okay." Rob shook his head. "But I've thrown an awful lot of rocks, and it never bothered me before."

"It's not the same," Carl said. He looked around at Tom. "When are the tryouts?"

"Today at noon."

"Not much time." Carl looked down at his brother's feet. "You need a glove and spikes."

"Can I borrow your glove for today?"

"Sure, but there's no way you can use my old spikes. We'll probably have to go off-Island. What size are you wearing?"

"Fourteen."

"Those aren't shoes, they're dinghies."

Rob laughed. "Catch you later," he said, and he and Tom walked to the Jeep and climbed in.

"I'm glad you've got the top up," Tom said.

"What a wuss. It isn't even cold."

"Cold enough," Tom said.

"It'll be a lot colder in Amherst."

"Yeah, but the baseball team goes south then."

They headed out the drive, downhill to Middle Road, and then over to the Coast Guard station in Menemsha.

Chief Platt, a man of middle height, but with big arms and wide shoulders, greeted them from behind his desk as they walked in. "What can I do for you?"

"I wondered if there'd been any reports of boats blowing up," Rob said.

"Not that I know of," the chief said. "Why?"

"I found some stuff floating off Spring Point."

If these had been summer kids, he would have discounted it entirely, but they were Islanders and they'd grown up around boats. "What did it look like?"

Rob gave him as accurate a description as he could.

"Where at Spring Point?"

"Northeast, by now. Probably stuck on the beach."

The chief nodded. "Okay, thanks," he said. "I'll send somebody to have a look." He pulled a pad toward him. "Give me your number, Rob, and I'll let you know what we find."

Throwing Smoke

3

Rob sat on the bleachers with the kids who had come to try out, feeling very much out of place, as he listened to Mr. Harden, the coach, instructing the players who had returned from the year before, the guys who were the very center of the crowd he had always wished he were part of ... the jocks, the heroes, the guys that got the girls. He knew them all because Tom Kincaid was his best friend, but the irrefutable fact was that where the ticket to ride said, "sports," his had never been punched.

Heck, he thought, I would have left me out. I haven't got a single thing to recommend me, as far as anyone knows. Fair student, not a jock, no school activities. As Hemingway said in that short story ..."nada, nada, pues y nada."

Nobody asks a cipher, a nil, a zero to join their group. The only good to come out of all that, Rob thought, was that it didn't piss him off. It had never pissed him off. The most he felt was disappointed that he had not been included. Well, that wasn't altogether true, he thought. It was only since he had suddenly, inexplicably started to grow that he'd discovered a sense of perspective.

The word for what he felt was droll. It described his reaction to how his situation had changed, girls who had always treated him like some kind of harmless mascot suddenly had to recalculate, and lacking the guile to hide their surprise, they were left to cover their discomfort by chattering like wind-up toys. Girls ... go figure ... why couldn't they just act like people?

Droll. Stay with droll. Like now, comically ironic. Here he was, in a group of freshmen and sophomores, all of them, with perhaps a few exceptions, wondering who he was, most guessing he was probably new to the Island, and probably a threat in matters of making the team because he was so tall.

For the first time in his life, he was the tallest in a group of guys, and he felt as full of himself as a dog that's just rolled in vintage dead fish.

He was also the only one filling out a form because everyone else had taken care of that weeks before. Mr. Harden sent the team onto the field to begin warming up and the rest of the kids he sent to the sidelines to warm up their arms.

Rob finished the form, took it over to Mr. Harden, who also taught math, and handed him the single sheet of paper and the pencil. He hoped the guy coached baseball better than he taught math, because he was a terrible math teacher. What math Rob had learned, he learned from the book. He took a deep breath. That wasn't going to work here because baseball didn't come with a book.

"So, Rob, tell me," Mr. Harden said, "what made you suddenly decide you're a ballplayer?"

Rob grinned. It was a reflex, a trick he'd learned years ago to disarm people. "I never tried out for a team before, and this was the only one left."

Harden grunted. "It says here you want to be a pitcher." He was several inches shorter than Rob and his stomach stuck out over his belt. He wore a gray practice uniform, spikes, and a cap pushed back on his head. "Is that right?"

"Yup."

"And you've never pitched before."

"I threw some this morning," Rob said.

Harden smiled and in his mind he wrote Rob English off. This was a joke of some kind, that's all. "You got spikes?"

"Didn't have time to get them this morning."

"How about a glove?"

"I borrowed my brother's."

Coach nodded. "Okay, Rob," he said, "the way it works, everybody gets a fair chance. Go warm up."

Rob picked up a ball and walked back to the worried looking sophomore and freshmen pitchers and catchers. Off to the south he could see the smoky dark of the fog beginning to move in as it always did this time of year when the air grew warmer than the water.

Nobody spoke as they tossed the balls back and forth like robots. Out on the field they could hear the regular players laughing and carrying on, and it made him feel even further away from any chance of making the team.

They'd been at it about fifteen minutes when Mr. Harden shouted: "Okay! Everyone! Two laps around the field and then we'll get down to business."

And that produced another surprise. He could run faster than he ever had before. Not that he was particularly swift, but now his long legs carried him easily along in the middle of the pack. Before he would have been pumping like a basset hound to keep up.

They gathered inside the backstop, Mr. Harden standing on home plate. "Okay, here's the way it works," he said. "Go out and take the position you want and we'll hit some balls to you to see how you can field. In the meantime, we'll start batting practice. When it comes your turn to hit, you get ten pitches and out. Run the last one out no matter where you hit it. Fair or foul, they all count. All of you pitchers and catchers meet behind the backstop with Tom Kincaid and Wally Wilson and start warming up. "We'll bat through twice so everybody gets a good chance to show us what they've got. Okay, get to it."

Rob walked around the backstop where Tom and Wally were waiting, both of them with their catching equipment strapped on.

"You wanna go first?" Tom asked.

"Naw. I'll wait."

Tom laughed. "Getting nervous?"

"Nope."

Tom looked at Rob carefully, sizing him up and then he shook his head. "You really aren't nervous, are you?"

"Nervous is when Carl has a hundred bucks riding on whether I can hit the stone," Rob said.

"Did you ever miss?"

He grinned. "You always miss the first two."

"Sucker 'em in."

"Makes the stakes go up."

"How is it I've known you all my life, and I never knew you were a hustler?"

"Carl's the hustler. I just throw the stones."

Tom laughed and looked over at the pitchers. There were six of them not counting the starters from last year. One of the starters, Walt Sewicki, was already warmed up and ready to throw batting practice.

"Wally will warm up whoever's next on the mound," Tom said. "I'll catch the first half of batting practice. You other guys divide up and throw lightly. Each of you will throw to six batters." He turned to Rob. "The tall rangy guy here will go last, so he'll keep track of when we need to change pitchers."

"Thanks," Rob said.

"Hey, anytime, big fella." He tapped him on the shoulder with his mask. "Get ready." He trotted on around the backstop.

Being tall, Rob decided, was gonna take some getting used to. Never in his life had anyone ever called him "big fella." It was something he thought he could grow to like.

He divided his time between watching the pitchers on the mound and the pitchers warming up, and he wasn't impressed. The guys from last year's team could throw, but not all that hard, and the newcomers were green. Only one had any speed, but he was wild, and Rob had to put a guy behind Wally to catch the ones that went over his head.

And all the time the fog came closer, and he began to wonder if he'd even get a chance to pitch. With just one guy left ahead of him, the fog hung like the smoke from a brushfire. It was gonna be close.

Tom finished warming up the next pitcher and stood up. "We'll just make it," he said as he waved his glove up at the fog. "Okay, kid," he said, "go throw some strikes."

The kid was so nervous all he could do was swallow and nod and head for the mound.

"This won't take long," Tom said.

"He isn't very fast."

"All he can do is throw it over the plate."

The six batters flew by and then Rob headed for the mound and Tom took over behind the plate.

"What's up?" Wally asked.

"I don't think you wanna catch him," Tom said. He pulled the extra piece of sponge out of his back pocket and stuffed it into his glove.

"Who? Rob?"

"Yeah, Rob."

"What've you been smoking?"

"Just watch."

Tom squatted down behind the plate as the first batter stepped in. Mr. Harden turned to see who was on the mound and then looked away. Behind his mask Tom grinned as he held up the target. This was gonna be fun.

Rob rocked into his motion and then seemed to explode forward, his arm coming right over the top. The ball hit Tom's mitt dead center with the smack that only a real fastball makes. And that got Mr. Harden's attention.

The next pitch came in belt high, only it was faster than the first one. The ball was in his glove before the batter swung. Now everyone was watching, especially the three pitchers from last year, who were suddenly facing some competition.

After the fourth pitch, Mr. Harden was standing behind Tom, watching him move the target to the inside and then to the outside and then back over the plate, and wherever he held the glove, Rob hit it. The batter had no chance at all.

"Okay, give me another batter here," Mr. Harden said. "Pinkham, get up here and see if you can hit this guy."

Pete Pinkham had led the team in hitting for two years and last year he had started hitting home runs. He was six feet tall, broad shouldered, and quick. But he was no match for Rob English. No matter how soon he tried to start his swing, he simply couldn't catch up to that fastball.

He stepped out of the box, looked back at Mr. Harden and then out at the mound. "Hey, Rob, where you been hiding all this time?"

"I was a dwarf, remember?" The laughter was general, and even Mr. Harden laughed.

"Okay, men, that's it for today." He stepped away from the plate and looked up at the fog which had now begun to drop like a curtain on a stage. "I'll post a list Monday afternoon for the first cut. Second cut is next Friday."

Rob walked over to the bench where Tom was packing the catcher's equipment into a duffel bag. He picked up the shin guards and handed them to him one at a time.

When he'd packed the bag, Tom stood and slung it over his shoulder, carrying it by the wide strap on the side.

"You're kind of quiet," Rob said. "That a bad sign?" They began walking very slowly toward the locker room.

"What are you talking about?"

"The team! Did I make the team?"

"You know, I thought when we were out at your house, that maybe it'd be different when you had to face a batter, because that's when most guys fly apart. The pressure's on then. You have to throw the ball over the plate, and throw it where the guy can't hit it." He grinned. "That's when batters get hit, or the pitcher throws it over everybody's head. But instead, you got better. How do you do that?"

Rob shrugged. "I just don't get very excited, I guess." He looked down at the glove and then socked his left fist into the pocket. "You didn't answer my question."

"I can't. Only Mr. Harden can answer that."

"But what do you think?"

"I think you made the first cut. The next one is tougher. We'll have at least two inter-squad games and you'll get to work at least two innings in each game."

Just then Mr. Harden caught up with them. "What do you

think, Tom, should we keep him?"

"Hey, can't hurt to have another pitcher."

"Yeah, exactly my thought." He clapped his hand on Rob's shoulder. "Okay, Mr. English, you just made the team."

"All right!" Again Rob smacked his fist into the glove.

"But I'd like to know," Mr. Harden said, "where you learned to throw like that. "

"He throws stones," Tom said.

"Stones," he shook his head, clearly not believing what he had heard. "Just stones...."

"He can throw one stone in the air and break it with a second stone. I saw him do it, Coach."

"You can do that?"

"It took a lot of time before I got it down."

Mr. Harden shook his head. "Stones.... I don't believe it! You haven't played baseball anywhere?"

"No."

"And where do you throw these stones?"

"Anywhere, but mostly at Stonewall Pond."

Mr. Harden nodded. "Good place. There's more stones there than anyplace on the island." He took off his cap, scratched through his thick black hair, and then wound the cap down onto his head, leaving the brim tilted upward. "You do this a lot?"

"In the warm weather, probably seven hours a week."

"But how did you know where to throw the ball when you were facing Pinkham?"

"Tom gave me a good target."

"At least twice you shook him off."

"I wanted him to set up the outside corner."

"How do you know how to do that? How does someone who's played no baseball know that?"

"I watch the games on television. I was too small to play so I watched. 'You can learn a lot,' as Yogi Berra says, 'just by watching.' "

"Have your father and Carl watched you pitch?"

"Just this morning."

"And what did your father say?"

"He's putting me on a regimen ... so many pitches a day, time with the weights, running, that kind of stuff."

"Good. I'm glad to hear that. He knows what to do. He was a pretty darn good pitcher himself."

"So I've heard," Rob said.

"And Carl could hit. He could flat-out hit. I was surprised he only played that one year over on the Cape."

"He likes building things."

"How about you? Where will you be next September? College?"

"I never got around to putting in any applications."

"Why not? Don't I recall that you had a B in both Algebra One and Two?"

Rob nodded. "But the rest of my grades are mostly C's and nobody told me about signing up to take the SATs."

"Nobody told you?"

"I thought you just showed up and took the test. It's okay. I never could see why everybody was going to college anyway." He laughed. "But when I was a dwarf I couldn't see much of anything ... especially in a crowd."

He held the door and Tom stepped through carrying the bag and Mr. Harden followed.

"Your grades okay to play ball?"

"I've never had lower than a C in anything."

Mr. Harden nodded. "Here's what I want you to do. Throw tomorrow, but not too hard, just enough to get loose, and then ice down your arm. Monday you'll pitch at least two innings. Thursday you'll pitch a couple of more. Between those days, in practice, you'll run wind sprints and work your legs on the Nautilus. I'll give you a list of instructions on Monday. But the thing is, Rob, don't throw hard. Always give your arm time to recover. You threw thirty pitches this afternoon and some this morning and that's enough for now." Again he clapped him on the shoulder. "Now get showered up. I got some things I need to talk to Tom about."

From the second he entered the locker room he knew his life had changed, and he even knew why. He was one of the big dogs in the pack. Simple as that. He found it amusing to have risen so high so quickly. Certainly, he thought, this could be mined to some advantage. He could use this to settle old scores, to get back at the guys who had put him down, and it was very, very tempting. But nothing more. Just temptation, and Rob was very good at resisting temptation. He smiled to himself. Besides, he thought, I don't know how to act like that. I'd have to learn how to act like a jerk all the time. And what would be the point? To put someone else down? What would I gain? Nothing. No, that's wrong. I'd gain an enemy. Nobody needs enemies. And anyway that was all in the past now. What was done was done and you went on from there.

He opened the locker and started peeling off his clothes. Clearly, he thought, it is a fool who creates his own enemies. Right. No question. A fool. But wasn't it only fair that he get the chance to even things out with someone like Sam Bednarz? After all, the guy had been making fun of him and pushing him around since the sixth grade. He stood up and walked toward the shower room, the towel slung around his neck. Of course, attacking Bednarz could backfire pretty easily because the guy weighed about two-fifty and he lifted weights by the ton instead of the pound.

Clearly, any ideas he had of revenge would have to be thought through very carefully. To be sure, revenge tasted sweet, but if he got into it with a guy like Bednarz, all he'd be tasting was his own teeth.

A Puzzle With No Pieces 4

On Saturday night in the off-season you headed down to Oak Bluffs to hang out because what happened would happen in Oak Bluffs, except that it seldom did. So you went to the movies, got a pizza, cruised around a little, went home, and complained about how there was nothing to do.

Every week somebody drank too much beer and got sick, or somebody got too stoned, and either they got nailed by the cops, or got lucky and didn't get nailed by the cops, and then after a while the guys who had girls drifted off to their cars. But no matter what, you went to Oak Bluffs on Saturday night. That's why he was there, sitting in his Jeep, watching kids drift past, wishing that Tom hadn't gotten so tied up with Melissa. He wondered if you called it jealousy in a situation like that. Was he jealous of Tom or Melissa? Or both? Whoa. Slow down, fella, he said to himself, it's questions like those that end up making a guy think, which is a very dangerous business because that's how you end up being an adult, whatever that means. Worse, they make a guy who hasn't got a girl feel kind of sad, especially now in his senior year when everybody seemed to have paired up. On the other hand, things did seem to be changing in the girl department these days. At least they looked at him now.

Pete Pinkham strolled up to the open side of the Jeep. "Hey, Rob, what's up?" The three guys with him stood back on the sidewalk, looking at him curiously, wondering why Pinkham was talking to a nobody. After all, this was Rob English, and nobody had ever paid any attention to him.

Rob understood. He could hardly believe Pete was talking to him. Not only was Pete the most popular guy in the place, Rob thought, but this afternoon I made him look pretty bad at the plate. All he could do was go along with whatever Pete had in mind. If it was a put-down, he could deal with that. In the long run stuff like that didn't matter. "Nothing," he said, "dead as a day-old fart."

Pete laughed.

"Unless you count the fact that Roy Ord got blasted and blew like a whale all over the front window of Donny's Pizza. They had to come out with a hose to wash it into the street." He laughed. "Nasty. Very, very nasty."

Pete shook his head. "So's Donny's pizza," he said.

They laughed together.

"How come I never hear any big drinking tales about you?" Pete asked.

"Two beers and I'm flying like a summer kite," Rob said.

"Bummer."

"At least I won't get nailed by The Ultimate Onager."

"That guy is an ass, even for a cop." He took off his cap and ran a hand over his closely cropped red hair.

"You got a pretty good reputation for partying," Rob said.

"Only in the summer. No sports."

Rob tossed his head in the direction of the other three guys. "How about Dylan, Frank, and Ernie?"

"Not when they hang out with me. No booze. No drugs, especially no drugs. Harden would throw me off the team, and I've got a nice fat scholarship to B.C., and I'm not gonna lose it over something stupid." He slapped his hand on the door post of the Jeep. "We're walking out to the beach, you wanna go?"

"Yeah, sure." He climbed out of the Jeep.

"Damn," Pete said. "You sure got tall in a hurry."

Rob grinned. He could simply not get enough of hearing people say that. "My grandfather did the same thing," he said, "and he wound up being six-four."

They joined the other guys and headed up past the Flying Horses Carousel, shuttered for the season like so many other places on the Island. He liked the shutters. It meant the summer people had gone, allowing the population to shrink back to the people who lived here year-round. But even that number was growing, and he resented the change simply because he'd been born here.

"Hey," Pete said, " I heard Deb Parks got knocked up."

"Yeah," Dylan Riley said, "I heard that last week."

Pete laughed. "How come nobody ever told me?"

"'Cause you're never around, Pete." Dylan said.

"Yeah, Pinkham, if you did something except hang around the batting cage, maybe you'd know what was going on," Ernie Feldman said. He was big, a middle linebacker with arms like tree trunks. He had curly hair and nearly black eyes, and he always looked like he was ready to fight, though Rob could not think of a single time he'd heard about Ernie getting into a fight.

"Fat lot of good it did me this afternoon." He clapped Rob on the back. "But maybe you guys haven't heard the news yet."

They all looked around, eager for any news.

"Ol' Rob here has suddenly come of age. He's got a fastball that nobody can believe. Kincaid had to use a double sponge in his mitt to keep it from killing his hand."

"What?" Feldman laughed. "Hey, no offense, Rob, but this has gotta be a put-on, right?"

"Nope." Pete shook his head. "I couldn't hit a single pitch he threw in the tryouts this afternoon, and every one of them was over the plate."

Rob looked around, absorbing the puzzled looks, reveling in them. Then he shrugged. "Made a deal with the Devil. I get to be a great pitcher and I have to give him any bass I catch over fifty pounds. Seemed like a cheap price to pay, considering that I've never caught one over forty."

They laughed and then Feldman spoke up. "Seriously, Pete, can he really pitch?"

"Come watch the inter-squads this week. Nobody will put a bat on the ball."

But it was still not a piece of news they could believe. It was just too outrageous. Nobody went from nothing to something without some kind of warning. On the other hand it was very encouraging news, because if it was true, if a dwarf could grow, if a dweeb could rise to glory, then everybody had a chance.

"I just grew," Rob said, "and along the way something happened."

"Can you really do that trick with the stones?" Pete asked.

"How'd you hear about that?"

"Tom."

"Yeah, I can do that."

"I'd like to see it," Pete said.

"It's dark, Pete."

"How about down by the Ferry Pier, in the street lights."

"I never tried it except in daylight."

"Give it a shot."

"Okay." Rob figured he had nothing to lose. If he missed he could blame the dark. But if he pulled it off, he'd be a legend, and nobody missed a chance at something like that.

They trooped down to the beach below the ferry dock that reached out into Nantucket Sound. Rob found a couple of rocks: a lump of white quartz to throw first so it would show up in the light and a nice round lump of granite.

"What's he gonna do?" Frank asked.

"Just watch," Pete said.

Rob looked out over the water. Always before, when there were people watching, he'd had Carl there to steady him. Now he was on his own. He took a deep breath and focused his mind on the stones, making a picture in his mind of the stones as they collided. And when he had the picture perfectly clear, he tossed the white stone in a high arc and then fired the second stone. It sailed in a perfect line, both stones shattering.

Stunned silence.

"Whoa," Frank said. He rubbed his pale blue eyes, looked out over the water, then looked at Pete. "Did I see what my eyes tell me I just saw? That was like, totally awesome!"

Pete laughed. "Why do you think I couldn't hit what he was throwing? This year we go all the way to the state championship. With me, Kincaid, Kelly, and McGivern hitting, and Rob pitching, we may be unstoppable."

"I gotta see that again," Ernie said. "Nobody can do that."

Rob shrugged, found two more stones, and repeated the stunt, noticing this time that at night the stone was lit on the bottom half instead of the top half. It made no difference.

"How do you do that?" Ernie asked.

"I don't know. I just do it." Something floating near the beach caught his eye and he walked toward it, kicked off his Topsiders, and waded out several feet to pick up three short planks. The ends were freshly broken, the wood still a pale tan in color, and the white paint on the outside had clearly been scorched. What was going on? Was this from the same boat? Had it run into a mine? No. Totally improbable. Or was it? Had the Navy lost a mine overboard? Maybe it was something left from the war.

"What you got?" Pete asked.

"Some boards from a boat hull," he said. "I found some more this morning way up toward Menemsha. I'll bet anything they're from the same boat." He handed one to Pete and the rest to Ernie and Frank. "What do you make of 'em?"

Pete's father was a fisherman, and Pete had spent a lot of hours on the water. "The boards are freshly broken and scorched on the outside, but that doesn't make any sense. If the boat blew up, the burn marks should be on the inside."

"That's what I thought too."

"Did you show them to anybody?" Frank asked.

"I told Chief Platt at the Coast Guard station and he said they'd take a look, but there was no report of any boat having blown up."

"Well, this boat sure as hell blew up," Pete said. He tossed the board onto the sand. "Were there any bigger pieces?"

"One. It was a piece out of the hull, just above the water-line. From the curve I'd say the boat was close to forty feet."

The voice from above startled them. "You boys having a nice time smoking your dope down there?" It was The Ultimate Onager.

"Yeah, right," Ernie said. "Why don't you come down here and toke up?"

"I'll get you one of these days," Onager said.

Dylan had his mouth open, ready to deliver one of his very best snide remarks, when Pete's big hand closed over his arm and stopped him.

"S'matter, afraid of the law?" Onager chuckled.

"Nobody wants any trouble, Onager," Pete said.

"I oughta just come down there and pinch you anyway. On general principles."

It was an empty threat and they knew it. Onager was so fat he looked like he belonged in a circus sideshow, and it was a long way down the steps to the beach. It would be a whole lot longer for Onager going back up. No one answered.

Out of the corner of his eye, Rob saw Dylan drop some pills into the water.

"Everything's cool here," Rob said. "We were just looking at some planks that washed up. Have you heard anything about a boat blowing up somewhere?"

"A boat? No. Nothing. And anyway, who cares? I'm out here to keep the roads clear of drunken teenage dopers."

The pills were dissolving very slowly and Rob thought if Dylan moved Onager might be able to see them. "Hey, can I call you later and see if anything came in about the boat? I told the Coast Guard about it this morning."

Onager shook his head and pushed back from the pipe railing. "Dumb boat." He waddled out of sight and they heard the door of the cruiser shut.

Rob stepped into the water, ground the pills into the sand, stepped back out, and picked up his shoes. "That was dumb, Dylan," he said. "If you had moved he could have seen that stuff from where he was standing."

"What are you talking about?" Pete asked.

Rob tossed his head in Dylan's direction. "He had some

kind of pills on him."

Pete whirled around and grabbed Dylan by the front of his jacket, twisting the excess material into a ball. "You had that on you? You told me you were clean!"

"I forgot all about 'em, Pete, honest. I forgot until I thought maybe he was gonna search us."

"What was it?"

"Speed. Just speed. That's all."

"You could've got us all arrested and my old man would have killed me!" Pete said. "I'm outta here...." He ran up the steps two at a time and the others followed, Dylan trying to apologize, but already knowing that he was now on the outside looking in. He also knew that it wasn't likely to change.

Nobody talked as they walked to the cars, Dylan hanging back. "Hey, guys, he said, "how about we set a trap for The Ultimate One. We wait for low tide and make a long trail of doughnuts down to that rotten pier in the pond. He'd go through about halfway out and fall into the mud, and this time of year he could holler forever and nobody would hear him until morning."

Pete stopped. "That was funny," he said. "Hey, guys that was funny. I mean, I thought that was funny." Suddenly they were all laughing at the image of the big, fat Ultimate Onager stuck to his waist in some of the smelliest mud on the Island, hollering and hollering and sinking deeper.

"How many doughnuts would that take?" Ernie asked.

"Five or six dozen, I figure," Dylan said. "And they can be

any old doughnuts, nothing fancy."

"I think he likes chocolate cream best. One bite and he'd never be able to stop."

"All this talk about doughnuts," Ernie said, "it's making me hungry. I think we oughta go for pizza."

"Okay, then," Pete said. He looked around at Dylan. "You going with us?"

"I'm ready," Dylan said, the relief clear in his voice.

"How about you, Rob?" Pete asked

"Nope. Dad's got me on a training schedule. I'm supposed to be home by ten. And I gotta drive slow. Onager follows me everywhere."

"Why does he do that? I mean, why does he follow you?"

Rob shrugged. "Ever since I got my license he follows me. I never even knew who he was till I could drive. And now, every time I come down here he follows me like a bird dog on a hot scent." He climbed up into his Jeep and started the engine.

"Hey, man," Pete said, "take care of that arm."

Rob grinned. "See you Monday." He backed out and headed slowly out of town, and sure enough, a half-mile later he spotted Onager, parked in a driveway. In his mirror he watched the car pull out and follow him until he crossed over the bridge into Vineyard Haven. What is it with this guy anyway? Why is he on my case? I've never even gotten a ticket. In four years of high school, I've never been sent to the office.

It was a night for cops. They were crawling all over Vineyard Haven and they were even on patrol in West Tisbury. He grinned. Onager had done him a favor. Once you see a cop you drive at the speed limit and each time he went past one they ignored him. Not that there was anything new about seeing cops around, especially on a Saturday night, but still, it seemed like there were more than usual. They were looking for something and he wondered what. Then he thought about Sunday morning and fishing again over at Spring Point. Where one bass showed up, there would be others.

There was also the matter of church. It started at ten, which meant it conflicted with the tides, which meant he'd miss another of Reverend Parks' dull sermons. Mom wouldn't be happy, but what could she say? He hadn't missed a Sunday since the blues headed south in the fall, and the rest of the year the tides came first. And anyway, going fishing was as good as going to church, at least among the men in both sides of the family.

5

The Mystery of Fishing

After two solid hours of casting he hadn't so much as turned a fish. He'd gone through half the flies in his book, he'd fished at different depths ... but nevermind ... it was still better than being closed up in the church.

In truth, it just wasn't a good day for bass, too bright and hot, with only an occasional cloud drifting by. He hooked the fly to the keeper on his rod, pushed his way through the water and up onto the beach. If he weren't so stubborn, he'd have given up on this spot an hour ago. But once you caught a good fish in a place, you always wanted to go back.

He decided to try around the point. The tide hadn't much left to run but he thought he might get in a half hour. It was worth a try. Some of his best surprises had come that way, following a whim instead of carefully planning his strategy.

He pulled off his waders, put on his cross trainers, and with his waders draped over his shoulder, started around the point. He stopped just as he cleared the rocks, looking some fifty feet ahead at a pair of bare legs sticking out from behind a big gray boulder. Girl's legs. Nice girl's legs! He stood for several seconds, trying to make up his mind whether to walk past or turn back, and in the time he stood there, he noticed that the legs hadn't moved. That fueled his curiosity and energized his imagination. Was she dead? Was this a body from the boat? He walked on, moving faster, and just before the rock he stopped and stared at the legs. What if it *was* a body? In the silence with only the gentle fall of the waves against the sand, he could hear his heart beating like the thump from a big bass speaker.

They were awfully pretty legs, he thought. And then suddenly one leg moved, putting the toes in position to scratch the other leg, and he began to relax. But as he calmed down, his curiosity grew, and now he wondered who she was. Finding out would not be easy. He might be a lot taller, and he might be a ball player now, but when it came to talking to girls he was still only five-four. He glanced at the water twenty feet away, considering whether he could just walk on past. But wouldn't that look like he was afraid of girls? He grinned. He *was* afraid of girls. Not like good old Kincaid, who could just saunter up to any girl and start a conversation.

Maybe it was time for a change. After all, he wasn't all that bad looking, and now he was a ballplayer, and if Tom and Pete were right, he might even be a star, and stars could talk to girls. Yeah ... right ....

He took a deep breath and walked around the rock as the girl, hearing him now, closed her book, rolled over, and sat up.

"Hi," he said, getting the word out before what he saw could sink in and tie his tongue into a bowline.

"Hi."

She had long blond hair and hazel eyes and she was slender where girls are supposed to be slender and ... and ... well she was a complete package.

"Nice day for sunning." It sounded pretty lame.

"Beautiful," she said.

"Do you come here often?"

"Not at this time of year." He was, she decided, a lot better looking than her father had said, but then he never knew which boys were cute. "You must be the guy my father told me about."

He made the connection. "He's a nice guy," Rob said.

"My name's Mallory."

"I'm Rob."

She nodded. "Catch any more big fish?"

He grinned. "Too bright for fishing."

"I saw you when I came down to the beach."

Rob looked up at the sky. "Too bright," he said.

"Are you a senior?"

He nodded.

"Me too." She sat, leaning back against her arms. "What are you doing next year?"

He shrugged. "I haven't decided yet."

"Are you going to college?" She knew the answer, but she wanted to see how he looked when he answered.

"I don't think so." He looked away.

"Why not?"

"I just never thought about it. Nobody in my family ever

went." And then another thought occurred to him. Maybe she was going to the high school. "Where do you go to school?"

"Pomfret ... it's in Connecticut."

"How come you're here now?"

"Spring break. All my friends are off traveling, but I wanted to come out here." She smiled again, showing a lot of straight white teeth. "I wanted to relax, you know, read a few books and sit on the beach. We've been coming here almost eighteen years. Since I was born."

"Then you've been here as long as I have."

"But you live here, so it's not the same."

He nodded.

"What's it like in the off-season?"

"Quiet. Really quiet."

"And ... boring?"

"Lots of my friends say they're bored." He laughed. "It helps if you like to fish and hunt and read."

"I guess I'd be okay then," she said.

"Really? I mean, you fish and hunt?"

"I'm kind of a tomboy. But I haven't done much hunting because I've been away at school in the fall." She smiled up at him. "Am I the only girl you ever met who hunts?"

"And I don't know a girl who fishes either. I think that's pretty cool."

"Were you quitting?"

"No, I was heading up to the inlet." He pointed with his rod. "Sometimes the bass hang in there."

"Do you mind if I come?"

"No. I'd like the company." He wondered where the words were coming from. Maybe it was Mallory. She made it very easy to talk. "Do you fly fish?"

"Nothing but, with *my* father. He had four girls and he taught us all to fly fish, shoot, and play golf." She stood, picked up her blanket and book. "I hated it at first."

They started walking along the beach, keeping to the hard sand. "But you did it."

"I'm the youngest. My sisters did it, and I wanted to be better than they were ... good old sibling rivalry."

"That didn't affect me too much," Rob said.

"Why not?"

"I was real short until this year, and my brother, Carl, was a heck of an athlete, but I was too short to play any sports, so there was no question of competing. But he can't handle a fly rod for anything, so I beat him there." He grinned. " I think maybe he let me win at that. I needed to win at something."

She looked up at him. "How short were you?"

"Dwarf short. In September I was five-foot-four."

"How tall are you now?"

"Six-two and I think I'm still growing."

"That's so strange..."

"Pretty strange," he said. "One time I grew almost an inch overnight. One day my pants were just the right length and the next day I was wearing high-waters."

She laughed. "Are you serious?"

"Yeah, really. It's true. I pulled my pants on in the morning and I looked down and I said, 'whoa, these pants have shrunk.' So I asked my mother if I had any other pants, and she didn't know what to say, except to call for my dad. He'd measured me just the night before because I was growing so fast, and he measured me again, and I was an inch taller. I mean, it was like a miracle. You now how when you're younger, you wish so hard for something to happen? Well, every hour of every day, all I did was wish I was taller, and then suddenly I was."

"And you're still growing?"

"Either that or my pants keep getting shorter all the time." He smiled as she laughed. "But I'm not growing as fast as before. If I stopped now, that'd be fine."

"That's so amazing."

He glanced around at her, smiling, pleased with himself at being able to make her smile. He didn't think he'd ever met a prettier girl, and certainly he had never met one who was nicer. "Where are you going to college?"

"Bowdoin."

"That's up in Maine, isn't it?"

"Uh-huh. Daddy went there."

"Where did your sisters go?"

"Janet went to Trinity, Lacy went to Conn College, and Marjorie went to Stanford ... she's the *really* smart sister. She wants to be a research chemist. She's so cool, I mean you'd think such a super student would be a real nerd, but she's not. In fact, she's the wildest one of us."

"It sounds like you get along with your sisters."

"Well, Janet's kind of a pain in the ass sometimes. She's the oldest, and she always has to tell everyone what to do, but she's getting married this summer so she won't be around, and Lacy is working in New York, so I don't see her that much either. But Margie is only two years older, and we have a great time."

"All my friends complain about their brothers and sisters but Carl and I always gotten along. I thought I was just weird."

"Why don't brothers and sisters get along better, I wonder? The kids at school have the same problem. There isn't one in fifty that gets along with the other kids in their family."

"Maybe we're just lucky."

"I guess, but it must be more than just luck."

"Most things are," he said. "But luck sure helps."

"Like when you're fishing."

"Yeah. If the fish aren't there, or they aren't taking, you get skunked. I used to hate that. But after a while, I just liked being free to fish, with nobody to bother me. Hard to beat that."

"All I worried about was that I'd come home from fishing, and go out on a date smelling like fish."

He laughed. "Now, that'd be my kind of girl."

She pushed against his shoulder. "Rob! No girl wants to hear something like that!"

"How would I know? I've never been on a date!"

"What?"

"Not one. Nobody wants to go out with a dwarf."

"And you're planning on making up for lost time, right?"

"If I wasn't so scared."

"Of girls?" She shook her head. "You don't act like any guy I ever met who was scared of girls."

"You're pretty easy to talk to, Mallory."

"Why, thank you. That's a very nice thing to say."

He pointed toward the end of the beach with his rod. "The water's deep, close in to the shore there. It's a good place to fish." He grinned at her. "You want to try?"

"Sure."

"You won't even have to wade."

"You're sure you trust me? It's an awfully nice rod."

"Not even worried," he said, though that wasn't altogether true. It was the most money he'd ever spent on anything, and he was very proud of owning such a fine rod, yet, clearly, it was a risk he was willing to take.

They stopped where the sand began to give out and the shoreline curved inward into the small bay. Rob laid his waders over a rock and then handed Mallory the rod, their hands touching briefly.

She turned and smiled at him. "Do I get some instruction?"

"I hate to tell anyone how to do anything," Rob said.

"Really? Most guys I know love to tell girls what to do."

He shrugged. "I hate to be told what to do."

"Let me tell you what I don't know, then. First off, what are we fishing for?"

"Striped bass," he said.

"Nearly all the fly fishing I've done has been for trout."

He pointed out to where the water swirled around several large boulders. "Try the water around those rocks."

"Uh-huh."

"Throw the fly outside of the rocks, maybe twenty or thirty feet. Let the line carry the fly down to the bottom, then begin working it toward the shore. Make the fly dart and stop, dart and stop, just like a bait fish."

She smiled up at him, wondering why she liked him so much already. He was different from the boys she knew at school. And she didn't know anyone who wasn't going to college. "That wasn't so hard, was it?" she said.

"What?"

"Telling me what to do."

"No, I guess it wasn't."

"Just guess?"

"Well, I mean, you go to private school and you're going to college and all."

"Rob, they don't teach fishing in places like that, you know."

He sighed and looked out over the sparkling blue of the water, off toward the Elizabeth Islands riding the horizon like an armada of purple ships. Then he smiled as he looked around at Mallory. "It seems sometimes as if all the growing up I've done has happened since last fall. It's like I had no life at all and then one day I did, but it's going so fast I can't catch up."

She looked up at him, differently now, her head cocked to one side. "I think you're already ahead."

"It sure doesn't feel like it." He wondered why he felt a

little down. Maybe there was something in what they'd said that had reached into him. For now, he let it go. He shook his head and smiled. "Ready to catch a bass?"

"Sure." She unhooked the fly from the keeper, stripped line from the reel until the long leader was well beyond the last guide on the rod, and then began to cast.

Rob couldn't believe it. Not only could she handle a fly rod, but her timing and the way she extended her arm to shoot the line forward to get the most distance from the cast told him all he needed to know. She knew what she was doing

"That was perfect," he said as the fly dropped onto the water beyond and outboard of the boulders.

For a half-hour she worked, casting over and over, and changing flies from time to time, but if there were any bass there, they weren't taking, and finally she wound in the line.

"Your turn," she said as she handed him the rod.

"Another day," he said. "Maybe tomorrow."

"I'm going back to school tonight."

"Whoa, there's some bad news."

"I've still got 'til the four-thirty ferry. Why don't you come up to the house for lunch?"

"Really?"

"Sure. You already know Daddy, and I'm sure Mom would like to meet you."

He seemed surprised, as if the idea that anyone would want to meet him was completely foreign. "I ... ah ... I don't know, Mallory, I mean I'm not dressed for much but fishing."

"And I'm dressed for sitting on the beach, and I have no intention of changing."

"Okay, I guess, if that's all right, then I'd like to." He wondered if he had ever understated anything so thoroughly. Of course he wanted to! He wanted to spend every second with her. "Thanks."

"And you don't have to worry. We're not the least bit stuffy. We don't dress for dinner, and we don't have servants, like some people who summer here. My mother does the cooking, and whoever's home helps, and Dad helps clean up."

"Sounds like home, except for the cooking," Rob said. "I can't cook anything."

"Does your Dad cook?"

"He's a great cook. Makes the best clam chowder that ever was. Maybe I'll have him teach me."

"Ask your mother too."

He picked up his waders, threw them over his left shoulder, and switched the rod to his left hand, and then, as his eyes swept the water, a life preserver caught his eye. What made his jaw drop, though, was the body in the life preserver.

She saw his expression change and she whirled around to look out at the water and then she saw it too, floating maybe sixty feet away. "Oh my God!"

He reached for his shirt pocket, unbuttoned the flap and pulled out the cell phone his mother insisted he carry when he went fishing alone. Quickly he punched up 911.

6

The Sea Casts Up Its Dead

He handed her the phone and unhooked the fly. With several quick false casts, he released some seventy feet of line, keeping it all in the air until the final cast, and then he shot his arm forward and the line snapped out through the guides on the rod, the fly landing well beyond the body.

He took the line in slowly, and when the fly reached the body, he set the hook, driving the point into the life vest. He reeled in the slack and slowly the body turned and began to move toward them through the clear water.

Fear and fascination held them as if their feet had been cemented to the sand. But when the body came within forty feet the emotion that dominated, at least for Mallory, was revulsion. All she could see was the dried blood but it was enough.

"Oh, God," she said as she turned quickly away, her face buried in her hands. "I think I'm gonna be sick."

Rob pulled the body to the beach, grabbed onto the vest, and hauled it partly up onto the sand. He cut the hook from the vest, took her arm, and they walked back up the beach to sit with their backs to a rock, looking away from the body.

"Are you okay?" he asked.

'"I don't know," she said.

He put his arm around her shoulders and she leaned in against him. "I can call your parents. Should I do that?"

"No," she said. "I'm okay. I'll be okay."

He said nothing, but continued to hold her, waiting for whatever would happen next.

Mallory felt safe with his arm around her shoulders. "I've never seen anything so awful."

"Me either," he said.

"Didn't it bother you?"

"Yeah, it did."

"But you still could touch it."

"I had to make sure it didn't drift away."

"No way could I have touched it."

"It's just what I had to," he said.

"Are you always like that?"

"I don't know what you mean."

"Like, taking care of business?"

"If something's got to be done, it's got to be done."

"But I was ready to panic and you just took care of things."

"It was no big thing, Mal ... is it okay if I call you that?"

"Everyone calls me that."

In the distance they could hear the sirens as the Chilmark police came roaring in over the Spring Point Road. Then there was a long wait while they ran down the beach, two of them: Don Crawford and Jane Turnquist.

"We'll have to talk to them," Rob said. "Can you do that?"

"If you hold my hand."

He smiled and with a boldness he had never imagined he possessed, he leaned down and kissed her on the forehead. "As long as you want me to hold you hand, I'll hold it," he said.

"Rob, that's so gallant."

As the police came closer, Rob stood, helped Mallory up, and then held tightly to her right hand.

"Hey, Rob," Don said, "did I get the message right? You found a body?"

"You got it right." He shifted his eyes toward Jane and then back to Don. "It's pretty ugly," he said.

Don, who was just two years older than Carl, nodded. "Jane, why don't you get a statement and I'll check out the body. The State guys and the Coast Guard are on their way."

"Okay," she said, relieved that she did not have to look at the body, at least too closely. It wasn't something the Chilmark police had done very often.

Then for some time, the place was crawling with officials asking questions, not so much about the body, but trying to find out if they'd found anything strange, or seen anything odd. Rob told them about the boards he had found floating the day before, and the Coast Guard guys corroborated what he said. They had even come over and picked up some of the wreckage.

Carrying the body away fell to the Coast Guard, because it was a lot easier for them to tow it out to their boat and haul it aboard with the gin pole than it was to carry it back down the beach. On most beaches they could have come in with any four-wheel-drive vehicle over the sand, but at high tide here they couldn't get past the rocks. The whole time he held her hand.

Rob and Mallory stood watching as the guys from the Coast Guard hooked onto the body and began towing it outward. Suddenly they heard a familiar voice.

"Mal? What's going on?"

She let go of Rob's hand and threw her arms around her father. "It was awful," she said. "We found a body!"

They walked back up the beach, Mallory telling her father again what they had seen, chattering excitedly as she tried to put the memory behind her.

"... And," she said, "I invited Rob for lunch. Is that okay?"

"Sure," Hal said. "We'd love to have Rob for lunch."

"Thank you, sir," Rob said.

Hal laughed and pointed at him. "Hey, it's Hal, right?"

Rob nodded. It had seemed perfectly natural yesterday to call him Hal, but it felt awkward now.

"I hear you made the baseball team," Hal said.

"Pretty amazing," Rob said.

"Not so amazing. I saw you throw, remember? I thought I might take in some of your games?"

"That'd be great," Rob said.

"Your coach tells me he never saw a kid throw the way you do, and I reminded him that you're not a kid. We have guys your age in the farm system for the Mets."

"Really?" Why had he talked to Coach Harden?

"Sure."

"Wow, the Mets...."

"But you're probably a Red Sox fan, right?"

"All my life."

Hal laughed. "Come on, we'll get some lunch. You gonna ride with Rob, Mal?"

"If that's okay."

"Sure. Just put your seat belt on."

"Dad...." she groaned.

"Only doing my job," he said.

He could count on one hand the number of times he had eaten lunch at anyone else's house, and every time it had been at Tom's. Suddenly all his mother's manners lessons began to pay off. Not that it was a formal meal, but he remembered to spread his napkin over his lap and to keep his right hand there instead of resting it on the table. And he used the butter knife to transfer the butter to the bread plate, and then managed not to gangplank his knife from the table to the plate, but set it crosswise on the plate. And most importantly, his vocabulary came well-salted with pleases and thank yous.

It was a lot to think about and still carry on a conversation but it helped that Mallory was so energized. She needed to talk, and he just let her go. But he was surprised that she got it all right, not because she shouldn't have, but because people seldom did when they told a story.

Mrs. Farrow, slender, with graying blond hair and blue eyes, seemed a little stiff, he thought, but when she asked him the sort of leading questions that mothers always ask, he managed to make her laugh, particularly when he referred to "my life as a dwarf." She seemed to appreciate his dry sense of humor.

After that she loosened up, though it wasn't clear to him whether it was his humor or the wine. Hal even offered him wine, but he turned it down, and he thought he scored well when he said he had to drive. It was even true. He did have to drive, and he never drank when he was going to drive. In fact, compared to a lot of the guys, he didn't drink at all. Mostly just a beer now and then when he was out fishing with Dad and Carl, and some summer six packs with Tom.

He never drank when he went out with Carl to make money breaking stones. Half a beer and he couldn't hit anything.

But then the famous question came up and it had begun to appear much too often lately.

"Where are you going to college?" Mrs. Farrow asked.

He knew he'd lose ground, but there was only one way to answer. "I didn't apply," he said.

"Are you going to work with your father?"

A yes would have been an acceptable answer, he thought, but it wouldn't have been true. "I don't know what I'm going to do yet," he said. He could tell by the look in her eyes that he needed something quick and funny to come back with, but he simply couldn't think of anything.

"Maybe," Hal said, "you ought to think about a year of post grad. It's pretty common these days. Us guys don't grow up as fast as the girls, you know."

"Education's not a major topic of conversation in my family. My father is the third generation of carpenters and boat builders in his family. Before that we were fishermen and before that whalers. The family's been here a long time. No one ever left." He finished his coffee and set the cup gently into the saucer. "Where would I go to do a post-grad year?"

"Anywhere," Mallory said. "We have a bunch of kids at Pomfret ...." She grinned and rolled her eyes. "Of course they're mostly big time jocks who forgot to study in high school."

"I qualify on the last part anyway," Rob said. "All I did was read. I mean, dwarves don't have much of a life."

"What did you read?" Mrs. Farrow asked.

Rob shrugged. "Novels, history, biographies."

"What books did you read?" Mallory asked, curious now at discovering another side of Rob English.

"Hemingway, Steinbeck, Faulkner, Dostoevski, Tolstoy, Melville, Poe, Crane, about a zillion mysteries and in history I read the Federalist Papers and biographies of Jefferson, Washington, Hamilton, and a whole lot of other stuff, especially on the revolution and the Civil War. Oh, and Shakespeare too."

"That's quite a list," Hal said.

"Which of Faulkner's books did you read?" Mallory asked.

"All of them. I get onto an author and I keep reading 'til I've read all of what they've written. Conrad. I forgot Conrad."

"I don't think I ever met anyone who has read all of Faulkner," Mrs. Farrow said. "His style is so, sort of ... turgid."

"If you read enough of him, it just becomes a style. When I

69

read *Light in August* the first time I really struggled. But by the time I got to *Sartoris* I just understood. My favorite is Hemingway, but not just because of the hunting and fishing. I like the way he leaves so much to your imagination."

He looked around at Mallory and then at Hal and Mrs. Farrow, and for a second he wondered whether he had committed some deadly *faux pas.*

"You read all of Shakespeare?" Mallory looked as if she didn't believe him.

"Shakespeare's a lot of fun," Rob said. "At first it's rough, but it gets easier as you read more."

"By God, Rob, you are truly full of surprises," Hal said. "Not only can you handle seventy feet of line in the air the way most good fly fishermen handle thirty, but then there's your trick with the stones, and from what I hear, a fastball that burns holes through the air, and now this."

Rob smiled. "I'm pretty deadly at video games too," he said.

"Where do you get the books?" Mrs. Farrow asked.

"Mostly from the libraries, and when they don't have something I borrow from people on the Island. There are a lot of very good private libraries here."

"Didn't any of your teachers say anything about college?" Mallory asked.

"I didn't get very good grades except in history."

"Did you take the SATs?" Mrs. Farrow asked.

"Nobody mentioned them."

"Why don't you take it," Mallory said. "Either that or the

ACT. I know that's coming up, because some of our basketball players need to qualify in order to play in college next year."

He felt stupid. He didn't know about any of this stuff. Why hadn't his advisor said something?

"Can you still get into college this late?" he asked.

"You can try," Mallory said. "And if you can't, then you can take a year of post-grad."

He nodded. "I could do that," he said. And he could, but somehow, he knew he wouldn't. It wasn't where he was headed just now, though he could not have said why he knew that, or even where he would go when school ended in the spring.

By the time they had finished lunch, Mallory had to pack to catch the ferry. She walked with him out to the Jeep, neither of them talking until they stopped by the door.

"If I write, will you write back?" Mallory asked.

"Sure," Rob said.

"Here." She handed him a slip of paper. "That's my address at school. How do I write to you?"

"Just Middle Road, Chilmark."

"Let me know what happens."

"With the body."

"Yeah."

He nodded. "It was the worst thing I ever saw," he said.

"But it didn't bother you."

"Pretty ugly." He shook his head.

"I think what you did was awesome."

"Awesome?" He shrugged, genuinely puzzled by her reaction. "I'm not very squeamish. I've cleaned a lot of fish and deer and rabbits, and blood doesn't bother me."

He was so unlike the boys she knew at school. So self-contained, so confident. What had he been like when he was short, she wondered?

"Daddy says you have a trick you can do with stones in the air or something. He was all excited about it yesterday. He said he'd never seen anything like it."

Rob looked down at the gravel drive, picked up a couple of stones, tossed the first one into the air and then whipped the second stone into it.

"My God! Did I just see that? That was incredible, Rob!"

He smiled and shrugged. "It was the only thing I had that made me unique...." He laughed.

They looked up as the door to the porch opened. "Mal, you're running out of time," her mother called.

"Okay, Mom."

The door closed and Rob opened the door to the Jeep. "I'll write to you," he said.

With no warning, she reached up and kissed him on the cheek, smiling as she stepped back. "Even with the sea giving up its dead, this was the best day I've spent in a long time." She turned and walked quickly to the house as he climbed into the Jeep and started the engine.

He drove slowly out over the gravel road, smiling to himself and thinking that finally his life was beginning to go the way life was supposed to go.

7

From Fastballs To Curveballs

Monday afternoon both his dad and Carl turned up to watch him pitch and Hal Farrow was sitting next to them. It was like being on stage, having to stand up in front of everyone and perform. No, this was better. At least he wouldn't have to say anything. All he had to do was put the ball over the plate ... right ... nothing to it ....

And to make matters worse, he was scheduled to start. Two innings. Just put the ball over the plate, and he'd only have to face six batters ... if he didn't have to stop and puke. His stomach felt like someone was stirring it with an egg beater.

He finished throwing the easy series of pitches at forty feet, and his arm felt loose and ready as he backed up to sixty feet, and finished warming up, gradually increasing his speed until he was throwing at maximum velocity. Still his arm felt loose, and he was on target, each pitch slicing the middle of the plate. He cut the right corner, low, then cut it high, then switched sides, and repeated it for the left side of the plate. Finally Tom stood up, the ball still in his mitt. "You ready?" he called.

Rob nodded and walked to the bench, slipping his jacket

over his left arm to keep it warm in the gray chill common to Martha's Vineyard in the early spring, when the sea stays cold and sends phalanxes of fog rolling over the Island. He looked up at the fog lying in a gray roll, still well off to the south. Now and then the sun shone a dull yellow in the smudgy gray of the sky, and then disappeared as if it had been blotted up.

"Okay," Mr. Harden said, "blue team take the field."

He dropped his jacket on the bench and walked out to the mound, bent over, picked up the resin bag, and dusted his pitching hand, and then dropped the bag on the backside of the mound away from the plate so no ball could hit it.

Tom threw him the ball, and he threw six more pitches, none of them hot. On the last pitch he signaled he was ready, and Tom threw to second base. Rob waited, facing third, as the ball went around, and then the third baseman, a freshman whose name he didn't know, tossed him the ball.

Whoa, this was just like the baseball he watched on television. Everybody knew what to do. He watched the first batter dig in. Sam Kelly: the third-best hitter on the team behind Pete and Tom, but he didn't have much power. He was a punch hitter who sprayed the ball to all fields. Tom had gone over each of the hitters with him, and while he didn't remember most of them, he made sure to remember the best ones because those were the guys who could do the most damage.

But not today. Today was his day. He went into his windup, never taking his eyes off Tom's big mitt, and then he started through, his left leg driving him forward as his arm came over at three-quarters and he let the ball go and followed through.

"Strike!" Mr. Harden hollered.

Sam shook his head and dug in, and Rob could see the muscles in his jaw bulge with determination.

But as good a hitter as he was, he couldn't catch up to Rob's fastball. It was in Tom's mitt before he swung.

"Strike two!"

The next pitch was no different, except that Tom called for it high, just at the letters, and Sam had no chance at all. Six pitches later Rob was sitting down, his jacket in place.

George English grinned as he looked around at Hal. "What do you think of that?"

Hal smiled. "He's got a great arm, George, no doubt about it. A great arm."

"He's the next Nolan Ryan," Carl said.

"You think he's throwing that fast?" George asked.

"Sure," Carl said.

"What do you think, Hal?" George asked.

He sat quietly for a minute. "When I first saw Nolan Ryan pitch it was in Double-A. I don't think he was as fast then as Rob is now. But Nolan got a whole lot stronger as he matured. Right now, Rob is faster. I think he's more accurate too."

"Sweet Jumping John McGee, ain't that something!" George English could hardly sit still. "Think of it, Carl! Poor skinny, short little Rob, who we've been worrying so much about all these years! It's almost too much to comprehend."

"He ought to be on a program," Hal said. "I know a guy

who I can get to come up. He's the pitching coach for the Triple-A farm team. He's pretty busy right now, but he'll come if I ask him. Would you like me to give him a call?"

"You're serious?" Carl said.

"Sure, I'm serious. Rob's got a great talent, but this is the most dangerous time. He's still growing, and that means everything keeps changing. The muscles stretch, the tendons and ligaments stretch as his bones grow, and he needs to learn to recognize the times when he shouldn't pitch. This guy is an expert at working with young pitchers. He'll design a program to fit Rob. The one thing you don't want to happen is to have him pull a muscle or maybe injure his rotator cuff."

"How much a fella like that will cost?" George asked.

"Let me worry about that," Hal said.

"We can't do that," George said. "It wouldn't be right."

"Oh, I'll get paid back. Rob's agreed to show me where to fish and information like that is as valuable as gold. And anyway, I'd just like to do it." Hal smiled, thinking of Mallory and how on the ride to the ferry all she could talk about was Rob English. He had never heard her so excited about a boy. She was always very picky, always finding fault, but the two of them had just hit it off, and he thought he'd like to help keep that going for as long as it lasted.

"Well," George said, "it's a very generous offer, and I'm in favor of such offers. For sure there's nobody here who knows things like that. At least I've never heard of anyone."

"I'll call tonight."

Rob took the mound again and nine pitches later he was through for the day and headed for the showers. He had walked all the way to the back door of the gym before he remembered that anyone had been watching. And now he wished that Mallory had been there to see him. Whoa ... calm down fella, he said to himself as he pushed through into the hall that led to the locker room. Just get a handle on this before you have to buy a bigger hat. Remember what it was like on the other side when the big jocks and studs treated you like a puppy dog. Never forget that.

By the end of the week it was clear that Rob was the first pitcher in the rotation. To be sure, there was some resentment on the part of the other pitchers, but they could not deny what they had seen. It helped that he did not change. He continued to be the modest, soft-spoken guy he had always been, and he laughed and horsed around, snapping towels in the locker room, trying to become part of what he had been outside of before.

That his best friend was Tom Kincaid, one of the stars on the team and every other team, helped considerably. He was riding high, sailing along as if cushioned by a cloud, and it worried him. It was too good. It was not the way things worked. But then in the mail on Friday he got a letter from Mallory and life only got better. He sat down the moment he'd finished reading it and wrote her back. He was so excited it was hard even to write, but then this was the first letter he'd ever written to a girl (or to anyone for that matter), and it was the first time he'd ever gotten a letter from a girl (or from anyone for that matter), so he was wound tight as a bluefish in a feeding frenzy.

He wrote with care, just as she had written, keeping the tone warm and yet neutral. It wasn't what he wanted to write. He wanted to tell her how much he liked her, and how pretty she was, and ... and ... well, a lot of other things too, but he didn't want to frighten her off either. So he kept to safe ground, talking about fishing and baseball, and how much he was looking forward to seeing her again, and asking when she would be coming back, even if just for a weekend.

And then it came time to sign it. He looked at the way she had signed her letter. "Your fly fishing friend, Mallory." It wasn't what he'd hoped for in a closing, but common sense said she couldn't have done anything more. Just keep it friendly and warm. No commitments. After all, they'd only spent a few hours together. He grinned as he thought about her. If it hadn't been for the body, it would have been absolutely perfect. Damn! The body! He'd been so wound up with baseball he'd forgotten to call the police about the body! He looked down at the letter and wrote: "With warmest regards, Rob." He addressed the envelope, sealed it, and raced outside to his Jeep. There was still time to get it in the mail. She'd get it on Monday. He'd have written first if he'd known what to say but until he got her letter he just hadn't known. Who could?

He got to the post office just before it closed, and while he was nearby, he swung over to the police station. Don Crawford was sitting behind the desk, and he looked up as Rob pushed on through the door. "Hey, Rob, what's up?"

"Not much," he said. "I wondered if you found out anything about that body. I didn't see anything in today's Gazette."

"The state police are handling it," he said. "They handle murders, we handle traffic tickets." He sounded disgusted.

"How come? The body was found in Chilmark."

"The state cops think they know everything."

"Will they send you a report?"

"Maybe. Sometimes they do and sometimes they don't."

"Sounds pretty weird to me."

"Makes it pretty boring too. I always wanted to investigate a murder."

"Did you talk to the guys at the Coast Guard station?"

"About what?"

"About the boat wreckage I found."

"Nobody said anything about any wreckage."

"I found it Saturday. A big piece of hull, probably from a forty-footer. It was all scorched on the outside, like it had run into a mine or something."

"Damn! Nobody tells us anything. What did the Coast Guard say?"

"They picked it up. Do you think they told the state cops?"

Don shrugged and leaned back in his chair. "Probably."

"I'm going out to Philbin in the morning. I'll look around."

"How did you get a pass for Philbin?"

"Dad owns some property in Aquinnah. I fish there a lot."

"Lemme know if you find anything."

"Sure."

Don grinned. "I see you're coming up in the world."

"In more ways than one," Rob said.

"Still growing, huh?"

"Still growing."

"Who was that girl you were with? Man, she is a looker."

Rob grinned. "I just met her. Dad built their house."

"Summer people?"

"Not anymore."

"And what's this I hear about you being some kind of powerhouse pitcher all of a sudden?"

"I haven't even pitched in a game yet."

"Carl tells me you throw lightning bolts."

It made him feel especially good to know his big brother was boasting about him. "He's exaggerating 'cause he's my brother," Rob said.

"Well, whether he is or he isn't, I think half the Island will be there on Tuesday for the first game."

"Whoa, now that's scary."

"Think you'll be nervous?"

"Wouldn't you be nervous?"

"I'd probably piss my pants."

Rob laughed, trying to keep himself under control, because if ever he was in danger of suffering from a swelled head, this was it. Don wasn't afraid of anything. "I'll just pretend I'm breaking stones."

"Are you and Carl still working that con?"

He shrugged because, after all, it was probably illegal and Don was not only a cop but he was a very straight guy.

"I'd like to see that some time," Don said.

"Just a trick, that's all."

"Pretty good trick, I'd say."

He heard the suspicion in his voice, and decided to defuse it with a question. "What do you know about Onager?"

Don grinned. "The doughnut bag?'

"Yeah."

"He on your case?"

"I think so. I mean every time I go down to Oak Bluffs to hang out he tails me all over the place."

"The guy gives cops a bad name. There's a lot of rumors about him."

"Like what?"

"Just rumors, but in the summer down there ... well, it's not the same as it used to be. Lot of wild kids now and a lot of drugs floating around. I suspect you've heard about that."

Rob nodded.

"The problem is there's a lot of stuff going on right in the open and nobody gets pinched." He sat back in his chair, locking his hands behind his head. "You met Paul Bianca?"

"Nope. Who's he?"

"The new state cop. He's planning to come down real hard on drugs. He's really a bulldog about the stuff. Gonna be an interesting summer if he starts cracking down. A lot of influential people summer there."

"How much can one guy do?"

"Not enough without local help."

"I didn't think Onager was anything more than a ticket jockey."

"Don't underestimate him, Rob. He may look like a fat fool, but only the fat part of that is true."

"I just wish I could get him to stop following me around."

"There's some history here you may not know. When we were all in high school, before he began to fatten up, Onager was part of a bunch of guys that had it in for anyone from up-Island. They made the mistake of picking on your brother one night, and they paid for it big time. He is a very nasty dude in a fight."

"Carl?"

"Yeah, Carl. He's strong as a damn bear and he hits like a hammer. He pounded four of them pretty hard and Onager was one of them."

"So now he's got it in for me."

"Pretty good guess, don't you think?"

"At least now I know."

"So just keep your head down and drive slow. And when you go out to Philbin, drive extra slow. The natives are restless without any summer people to fill their coffers. Especially Belgeddes. He acts like Islanders are the same as summer people. He was an okay guy before he found out he was part Indian."

"Warning taken," Rob said. "And thanks, Don."

"Anytime."

Fishing

8

In the morning, in the last dark hour before sunrise, Tom pulled into the yard, loaded his fishing gear into the Jeep, and walked up onto the porch to help Rob with the rest of the gear.

"So, where we going?" he asked.

Rob stuffed the lunch and the cooler full of ice into the back of the Jeep. "I thought we'd take the boat."

"Whatever you say, man. You're the guide."

"I put in an extra fly rod in case you'd like some lessons."

"I think I'll stay with my spinning gear," Tom said.

"Whatever turns you on," Rob said, "but if you wanna be a pro, you gotta learn to fly fish."

"Damn, the sun isn't even up and already you're breakin' my stones."

Rob laughed and they climbed into the Jeep and headed for Menemsha.

"And besides that," Tom said, "you're the one who does the wussy fishing. Surf casting is for men. You gotta be strong."

"Now who's breakin' stones?"

"Gotta keep it even, man."

The boat was moored near the back of the harbor, along the narrow channel that ran past the fish houses and piers on the waterfront. It was kept fueled and ready to go, and in minutes they had loaded the gear and shoved off.

It was a good, solid boat, a fiberglass Jonesboro lobster boat, thirty-five feet long, with a Westerbeke 6 diesel engine. She could handle almost any seas, and she cruised at a nice steady twenty-five knots. In calm water she could make up to thirty-five knots.

Rob turned on the fan to vent the engine, even though it was only a problem with gas engines where the fumes built up and blew with the first spark if you didn't ventilate the hold.

It was a routine as old as he could remember. It never varied. Everything was done in order, right down to casting off the final line and pushing out of the slip and into the harbor. The tide was dead low and the water flat as Rob headed out of the creek between the two jetties, turned toward Dogfish Bar, pushed the throttle up, and let the engine roar.

"I always forget how fast this boat goes," Tom shouted over the roar of the engine. "It looks like any fishing boat until you hit the throttles." He looked back at the wake and the streak of froth from the propeller, white against the gray reflection of the gray, predawn sky in the water. "How fast are we going?"

"About thirty knots."

"I thought only Cigarette boats went that fast!"

"They go a lot faster. Some of the racing boats will do a hundred, but most of them top out at seventy to eighty. And they can do that in a four foot swell."

"Now that's a lot more than I needed to know."

"You can never know enough," Rob said.

For a while, simply because it was too hard to talk over the noise from the diesel, they just rode. Finally, Rob eased the throttles back to cruise to save on fuel, swung his heading to north north west, and settled into the pilot's chair. "I thought we'd try Quicks Hole," he said. "With any luck we might find some blues running, or we can troll for stripers."

"Sounds like a plan to me," Tom said. He looked off to the east. "Looks like we'll have the sun," he said.

"It'd be better if it was cloudy, but we're early enough."

"What's this I heard about you finding a body?"

"Yeah, over at Spring Point."

"When?"

"Last Sunday."

"How come you never said anything?"

Rob shrugged. "I think I was trying to forget about it. The guy's face was all smashed in. It was pretty ugly."

"Do they know who did it?"

"The state cops aren't saying anything."

"Must've been weird, huh?"

"Pretty weird," Rob said, and then changed the subject. "How are you and Melissa getting along?"

"I don't know."

"What does that mean?" He didn't know much about girls, but he thought that was one thing you could keep track of.

"I don't know, that's all. Sometimes she's hard to figure. Anytime I want to do something with you or with any of the guys, she gets all weird. It's like she thinks she owns me."

"Like how?"

"She just gets into a mood, you know? Like last Saturday I wanted to go down to Oak Bluffs, but we ended up at her house."

"That couldn't have been all bad." Rob looked up at the Elizabeth Islands out ahead of them, picked a spot between Pasque and Nashawena, and adjusted his course just slightly.

"All bad." He shook his head. "We even had to watch a girlie movie. Man, I hate those things."

Rob smiled. Between the body and the pieces of boat, he had felt as if he were on the edge of being in a movie. And then he remembered he hadn't told Tom about the boat either. "Did I tell you about the pieces of boat I found?"

"What is this? First you don't tell me about the body and then you don't tell me about a derelict?" He shook his head. "I don't know about you, Rob."

"I forgot a lotta stuff this week. My life kinda changed."

Tom grinned. "Tell me about the boat."

"I found pieces of a hull out at Spring Point when I was fishing, and when I went back to fish again on Sunday I found the body not too far away. I figure somebody blew up a boat and the guy I found was on the boat when it went up."

"You think that's how his face got smashed?"

"I think somebody beat the crap out of him, put him on the

boat, and blew it up."

"Whattya think? A bad drug deal?"

"Something like that, probably."

"Do you think it happened on the Island?"

"Naw. Nothing happens on the Island. But it's hard to say just where either. Stuff drifts all over the place out here. We get junk from Providence, stuff floats through the canal. Who knows? It depends on the winds and the currents, and in these waters the currents are random."

The sun had eased up over the horizon, and in the flash of sunlight he could see tiny dots of white in the air ahead. Gulls! There were gulls and they were feeding in the way they did when something big was chasing bait. Blues? So early? Was it truly possible? Of course it was. In the ocean anything was possible. It just meant that the water was warming sooner than usual. He watched the birds, gauging their movement by the bow of the boat, and then he corrected to a point well ahead of the flock, as he pointed at them. "We got birds working," he said. "Get your rod rigged. I'm gonna cut in ahead of the school."

There wasn't much chance of getting there before the fish quit feeding and went down. It was just too far away. But he resisted the temptation to increase his speed. He wouldn't gain that much, and sometimes the sound from the engine at high speed could send a school of fish down. Instead he sat behind the helm, enjoying the wonderful fine salt smell of the sea and the sticky feel of it on his skin, and he watched the birds growing larger and larger. Now and then he corrected his course so he would come in ahead of the school of fish, even as he waited for them to sound. But instead more birds arrived, and now he could see the fish cutting through the surface of the water, slashing into the huge school of bunkers above, the water leaping upward to flash in the sunlight.

He slipped in well ahead of the school, cut his engines, and let the boat drift. "You ready?"

"Yup," Tom said, not taking his eyes off the school of fish that now was moving steadily closer.

"You can start casting anytime." He strung his rod and tied on a big blue and white fly. "Let me take the stern," he said. "That way we won't get fouled."

Tom stepped toward the middle of the boat, watching the school of fish moving steadily toward them. When they were in range he let go, firing a Ballistic Missile far out away from the boat, letting it splash down, and then starting his retrieve.

The plug hadn't gone four feet before a blue swirled and Tom hollered. "I'm on! I'm on!"

Rob began casting, throwing thirty, then forty feet of line, shooting it out through the guides so that the final cast carried his fly some sixty feet from the boat. As the fly hit the water a blue hit the fly and broke through the surface, soaring in a long arcing leap before crashing back down in a great spray of foam.

"You did it again! Every time you find fish! I don't believe it!" Tom played the fish skillfully, keeping his rod up, the line taut, giving line only when he had to, and fighting to gain line each time the fish paused to rest.

"These are big fish," Rob said. "We're over ten pounds here." His rod was bent almost double as he let the fish fight against the power of the rod and the drag on the reel. Already he could feel the muscles in his left forearm tightening, a feeling he liked maybe better than any other he knew. He braced the fighting butt of the rod against his stomach to rest his arm, checking a long deep run, and then he began retrieving line.

All around them blues were coming out of water, chasing the bunkers into the air. The gulls swooped in to grab pieces of bunker left by the blues, but they didn't stay on the water long. That was the way gulls got eaten, because in a bluefish feeding frenzy anything that moves is a target.

Tom worked his fish close to the boat, able to get it there faster with a spinning rod, and then the fish ran again, and again Tom checked the run, leading him back, and then suddenly the fish was just swimming, and Tom picked up the gaff, reached over the side, slipped the hook under the gill plate, and hoisted the fish into the boat. "Damn this is a big fish, Rob!"

Rob wasn't watching anything but the fish he had on, feeling the tail beat vibrating in the rod, and when the pulse suddenly grew rapid, he increased the pressure, knowing the fish was going to jump. He snubbed the jump by throwing his rod to the side and down, turning the fish so all it could do was swirl and then sound, giving it no chance to throw the fly.

Rob was still fighting his fish by the time Tom had killed his, put it in the fish box, and loosed another cast. Nothing. He cast again, every nerve tuned, hot, ready to explode when a fish hit, but again he came up empty. "The school is moving!"

"Almost there," Rob said. He led the fish in, gaffed it into the boat, and set his rod in the holder and started the engine, leaving the fish flopping wildly over the teak decking. He whipped the wheel around, shoved the throttle forward, and the boat seemed to leap into the air. Within seconds he was ahead of the school, and Tom unleashed a long cast as Rob shut off the engine, killed his fish, unhooked it, and threw it into fish box.

"All right!" Tom shouted as he hooked up.

The school turned and came directly at them, and Rob dropped his fly out about fifty feet and started his retrieve, watching the bunkers streaking past under the boat. He let the fly sink a little deeper this time and it worked.

For the next hour they caught and boated blues until their arms felt dead. They had each landed five fish, and tired as they were they would have kept on, but suddenly the fish disappeared. For a while the gulls swooped in and picked up the pieces of bunker, and then finally they settled onto the surface of the water, a sure sign that the blues had moved.

Rob dipped the mop over the side and began washing down the cockpit, while Tom sorted the fish, repacking them so they were covered with ice.

"What time is it?" Tom asked. "I forgot my watch."

"Time to eat," Rob said. He started the engines, ran the boat into the lee of Pasque Island, and dropped the anchor about a hundred feet from shore.

Tom opened the lunch cooler and they unwrapped the fat bologna sandwiches and broke out the chips and Cokes.

"My fingers are so stiff they feel like claws," Tom said.

"Yeah, mine too."

"Man, oh man! We didn't get into a school like that all last summer," Tom said.

"There's nothing more fun than fishing."

"I can't believe the number of guys who don't fish. All they do is hang out and play video games."

"Some of those games are pretty cool," Rob said, "but they can't compare to this. They're only good for winter."

For awhile they sat on the floor of the boat, working their way through the sandwiches and chips. The sun was high now, and he had expected the wind to come with it but it hadn't. The water lay glassy smooth all the way across Vineyard Sound. Rob looked up over the stern as he heard a boat coming through the channel from the other side. It was a big Chris Craft, a cruiser with the after deck ten feet above the water. It was an old boat, but it appeared to be in pretty good shape. Probably just out of the yard for the season, judging by the brightness of the paint.

But he thought the engines sounded very rough, and there was far too much black oily smoke hanging out over the wake of the boat. Why would you paint the boat and not tend to the engines? Maybe they were just shaking it down, but it was a long way from any marina out here, and usually you tuned the engines in the slip so if something crapped out you didn't have to get a tow. The boat, moving at a snail's pace, turned and headed down along Nashawena, a hundred and eighty degrees away from them, bit by bit disappearing around the island.

It had been gone from sight for perhaps twenty minutes when they heard the blast, a solid deep thump, and a large plume of black smoke mushroomed high up over the island.

"Get the anchor!" Rob said. "I think that boat just blew up!"

He cut a straight line toward the smoke, running under full power over the flat water. They hadn't even crossed the channel before the smoke changed from a steady plume to a single black cloud, cut off at the base, drifting slowly southward. Even at full speed it took some time to get there, and by then only a bunch of debris floated lazily on the surface. There was no doubt in Rob's mind what had happened, and he switched on the radio. The Coast Guard in Woods Hole answered first.

Tom stood on the front deck, using the binoculars to look for either survivors or bodies, but all he could see were pieces of the boat bobbing in the smooth water.

Forty minutes later the cutter pulled alongside, tied up to them, and an officer crossed over into their boat.

"I'm Lieutenant Parker," he said. "Are there any survivors?" He was a wiry, very young-looking man, just under six feet, and he spoke very quickly.

"We've been scanning since we got here, but there was no sign of anyone." Rob said

"How many people were on the boat?"

"I couldn't tell," Rob said. "I didn't see anyone when it came through Quicks Hole, but with a cruiser it's hard to see."

Lt. Parker nodded. "Did you see it go up?"

"We heard it," Tom said. "And then we saw a puff of black smoke, and I pulled the anchor, and Rob started the engine."

"By the time we got here, there was just rubble," Rob said. "It's hard to believe a boat that big could go down so fast."

"Must have been a pretty big blast. How far away were you when you heard it?"

"We were anchored at Pasque," Rob said. "I'd guess the smoke went up a hundred feet, and then the boat must have gone down, because there was no more smoke rising."

"How big a boat was it?"

"What would you say, Tom? Forty feet?"

"All of that."

He took down their names and addresses. "We're lucky you were out here," he said. "This is the fourth boat in a month that's gone down."

"I found pieces of one over on the Vineyard," Rob said, wondering why the chief hadn't told him about the other boats. Not that it was all that odd. Nobody tells kids anything important.

"We've never found the others," Lt. Parker said. "Nothing but debris ... and one body."

"Yeah, I know about the body," Rob said. "I was the one who found it."

"Now there's a coincidence," Lt. Parker said, and Rob wondered whether he heard just the faintest accusation in his voice.

Rob looked at the debris. "It must have gone down really fast the way the smoke stopped."

"We'll mark it and send the divers out," Lt. Parker said. "We'll find something this time."

"How come Chief Platt never told me about the other boats?" Rob asked.

Lt. Parker grinned. "Need to know," he said.

Rob grinned back. "Just like the spy movies, huh?"

"Something like that." He looked toward the fish box. "How was the fishing?"

"We hit a huge school of blues," Tom said as he stepped over and opened the lid. "We really got into 'em!"

Lt. Parker looked into the box. "Whoa, I guess you did! Kind of early for blues, isn't it?"

"Way early," Rob said.

"What made you decide to fish here?"

"He can't tell you," Tom said. "He never knows why he decides to fish in one place instead of another, but he always picks the right place."

"Well, not always," Rob said.

"The guy thinks like a fish."

Lt. Parker stepped up on the gunwale of the boat and then onto the low fantail of the cutter. "If I have any more questions I'll be in touch," he said.

They both nodded, unwound the lines from the cleats, and cast them off. Rob started the engine and they moved slowly away, and then, when he was a safe distance off, Rob pushed the throttles forward to cruise, and they headed for home.

Tom stood, leaning against the hatch to the cabin, making

it easier for them to talk over the noise from the diesel. "Hey, Robbo, I thought for a minute there he thought maybe you had something to do with all of this."

"So did I," Rob said.

"Talk about weird."

"Yeah, but I think it's more weird that Chief Platt lied to me. I mean, what's the harm, right? So I know about some other boats blowing up? You'd think it was a state secret."

"All the guys in the service are like that," Tom said. "My uncle Joe is a Captain in the Navy. He was in the Gulf War, but he won't talk about any of the cool stuff, like the missiles they fired. Classified. That's all he says, classified."

For awhile they rode, looking at the water and the Vineyard coming closer. Rob let the boat drift off to the southwest.

Tom looked at the compass. "Where we going?"

"I wanted to make a quick pass south of Dogfish Bar. See if anything's working. That school went somewhere and Dogfish is as likely a place as any."

"So's Wasque," Tom said.

"That's gotta be twenty miles from here. Too far."

It was a long quiet ride with the throttles set so the boat planed through the low swells without pounding. Out of the corner of his eye Rob saw a boat coming toward them and he guessed it must have come out of Woods Hole from the line of its wake, but he didn't pay much attention at first.

They made the swing outside Dogfish, cruising past the Gay Head cliffs and around the point of the land. He set the engine at idle and shifted to neutral while he got out the glasses and looked down along the coast. There were no birds working and if the fish had come this way, they weren't feeding.

"Nothing," he said. "Not a bird anywhere." He swung the glasses out toward Nomans Land, but he saw no birds there either. "Time to go home." He put the glasses away, put the boat in gear, swung the wheel, and pushed the throttle forward.

He picked up the boat again, watching it for several seconds, checking it against the compass before he recognized that the boat was on a constant heading with decreasing range. They were on a course to intercept. So? No big deal. Happened all the time; boats passing close because neither wanted to alter course. Except he had a strange feeling that this was something altogether different. He picked up the glasses and scanned the boat, thinking maybe it was the Coast Guard, but this was no cutter. This was a Cigarette boat, a big fast boat that could outrun almost anything, even in a heavy sea. It was the kind of boat favored by drug runners and it was headed right at him.

He decided to run. With his right hand he pushed the throttle forward and the diesel responded with a throaty roar as he brought the bow around. The boat leaped forward, slicing through the water as she dashed toward Gay Head.

"Are you crazy?" Tom shouted.

"See that boat?" Rob shouted. "It's trying to intercept us!"

"So what?"

"I don't know what. I just decided I didn't want him to."

"You're going through Devils Bridge, aren't you?"

"Yeah."

"You're gonna run aground, Rob!"

"I've made it before, and on a lower tide than this."

He ran at full throttle long enough so that no matter how fast the boat was it would not be able to cut him off before he raised the narrow cut between the bar and the beach. Off to his left he saw the Cigarette boat leap forward. It was bigger than he had thought, and he hoped he'd left himself enough room, because it was no ordinary boat. It was one of those sixty-foot monsters powered by huge turbo diesels and probably capable of hitting at least eighty knots, even in bad water. He looked down at his gauges and then at the water. That was one fast boat because he was making thirty-five knots, and he had by far the shorter run. It was gonna be close, and all he could do was hold his course and hope the guy driving the boat didn't know the water in close to the Island. Rob took dead aim on the inshore tidal rip where the waves ran six and eight feet at times; high choppy waves that no boat could take at high speed.

For what seemed like forever the boats angled toward each other and then, bit by bit, Rob knew he had the better angle and just enough speed to carry him into the cut first. And with a smaller boat, he could chop his throttles and maneuver around the rocks. He could see the pilot on the boat waving his hands as if he were arguing with someone, and then another man stood up and began pointing toward the shore and waving his arms. In the process, the Cigarette boat drifted just a bit off course, and that gave Rob another edge, another few seconds, and as it turned out, he needed every second.

Just fifty feet before the tidal rip, he chopped the power and cut the helm hard left, swinging the bow into the cut and pushing the throttle forward to get around the monster rock that lurked just under the surface. After that he didn't dare look back for the other boat. He was simply too busy navigating the cut through to the calm water on the other side. It helped that the tide was waning and the back curls in the rip were only a few feet high, making it easier to spot the rocks. In minutes he was through and into the calm water, and he hammered the throttle open, and went roaring down along Lobsterville Beach.

When he looked up the Cigarette boat had veered away, and stood well out to sea, heading dead north-northwest toward Cuttyhunk. He pulled back on the throttle, letting the boat fall back to cruise, and slowly his heartbeat returned to normal. He wondered what would have happened if he hadn't spotted the boat when he did. The shotgun was on board, housed in a locker just inside the cabin. Would it have come to that? Clearly, they had been chasing him, based on the way they had tried to beat him to the cut. But why? Because of what he'd seen?

Even by the time he slipped into the cut at Menemsha he was still pumped up, and to calm himself he followed the routines his father insisted on when it came to the boat, stopping first to top off the fuel tanks.

"Do you really think they were chasing us?" Tom asked.

"What do you think? You saw them turn when we did. If I hadn't been able to get through the cut, they'd have caught us."

"But why? Who the heck would want us that bad?"

Rob finished filling the tanks and handed the hose back up to Orwell Thomas. "Thanks, Or," he said.

Orwell wrote down the amount of the fuel and handed Rob the sales book. Rob signed it and handed it back to him.

"You guys get any fish?" Orwell asked.

"A few," Rob said.

"Blues?"

"Yup."

"You got blues this early?"

"Sure did."

"Where?"

Rob pointed toward Vineyard Sound. "Out there."

Orwell laughed. "Didn't think you'd tell me," he said.

"Quicks Hole," Rob said. "Big fast moving school."

"Might as well not have told me then," Orwell said.

Rob grinned and started the boat. They backed away from the pier and idled down to the pier at Larson's Fish Market.

It didn't take long to cut a deal and they sold off half the fish, leaving enough to freeze, smoke, and eat fresh, and then they idled down the long narrow harbor to the slip, tucked out of sight behind a bigger fishing boat.

They hauled the fish onto the dock and hosed down the boat and the fish wells before removing the gear. Finally, he checked the lines again, making sure they were properly tied, picked up his gear and the fish, and lugged them to the Jeep.

Already he was looking forward to his first bluefish dinner

of the season, and trying not to think about what had happened. Clearly, he was gonna have to tell someone, but he wasn't sure just who to tell. After all, it was a pretty wild tale, and when you were still only seventeen, well almost eighteen, adults were not inclined to believe anything you said, let alone anything as wild as this. He decided to write it all in a letter to Mallory and then think about what he'd do next.

"I think maybe we shouldn't mention this," Rob said.

"You mean about being chased?"

"Yeah. I think somebody must have heard us on the radio and they probably wonder how much we saw."

"So they came after us."

"Why else?"

"That's pretty scary stuff, Rob."

"It's the only reason I can think of. Guys in a boat like that sure weren't looking for blues."

9

Getting Help

He dropped the letter into the box, walked back to his Jeep, climbed in and sat, his hands on the top of the wheel, staring at the red, white and blue mailbox, worrying about what he had said in the letter to Mallory. All he'd talked about was baseball and fishing, and he had the feeling that he should have said something more, well, more personal. And then, on the other hand, maybe it was better not to have said anything too personal. Jeez! How did you even know about a thing like that?

He started the Jeep, backed around, and stopped at the road, checking for traffic. He stopped again at Beetlebung Corner but instead of going straight up Middle Road toward home, he turned toward Menemsha and the Coast Guard station.

Chief Platt was sitting at a desk going though some papers.

"Hi, Chief," Rob said as he stepped up to the counter.

The chief grinned. "I hear you found another one," he said.

"How come you didn't tell me about the others?" Rob asked.

"I hadn't cleared it with the Lieutenant."

Rob nodded. It was the answer he had expected. "Anybody know what's going on yet?"

"Nobody's told me if they do," the chief said.

"I wondered if you still had the wreckage from that boat."

"Sure. You want to look at it?"

"If it's okay."

"It's over in the boathouse. Follow me."

Rob followed in his Jeep, parking on the pier. He had never thought of Chief Platt as short, but he was; short and broad shouldered, and his hair was beginning to thin in the back. But no matter how tall he was, nobody screwed with Chief Platt. The story was that he'd been in several firefights with drug smugglers down in Florida before coming here, and he'd won them all. This was supposed to have been an easy tour, or so the story went. Waterfront rumors were usually pretty accurate, but when a guy had a reputation like the chief's, you had to wonder if maybe that was what someone wanted you to think.

They went through a door, and out into the big open maintenance area.

"We found it right where you told us," Chief Platt said.

Rob looked down at the section of hull and the other pieces scattered around. "Looks like you found a lot more too."

"It still keeps turning up. But we still haven't found anything below the waterline."

"Did the state cops look at this?"

"They asked me to send them a copy of my report when I finish my investigation."

"That's all?"

"I think they're more interested in the body."

"I can't believe they're not just as interested in the boat."

"But we are. The Coast Guard is always interested in boats, particularly in any boats that look like they were blown up."

Rob squatted down and picked up a piece of the hull. "What kind of boat do you think this was?"

"You tell me."

"Swanson."

"Pretty sharp, there, Rob. How did you tell?"

"By the way the planking is joined."

"Right again. Where'd you learn that?"

"Both my grandfathers still build boats."

"Did they build your boat?"

"We bought the bare hull and Carl did most of the work."

"What kind of an engine does she have?"

"Westerbeke 6. She'll do an honest thirty five knots."

Chief Platt grinned. "That's fast enough. Maybe not Cigarette boat fast, but fast enough."

"What do you think caused this?" Rob asked as he pointed to the wreckage.

"You can see the way I've got it laid out, right?"

Rob nodded.

"The same way they put together a plane after a wreck. But, as I said before, every piece is above the waterline."

Rob nodded. He was busy assembling a theory of why that might have happened. "The engines would have been aft of midships, so if the blast occurred ahead of the engines, the stern would have gone down like a rock."

Chief Platt smiled. "But there still would have been something from the forward section below the waterline. It was a big blast, big enough to have cut the boat in half."

"I don't know much about blowing up boats," Rob said.

"As it happens, I know quite a bit about that," Chief Platt said. "From what I can tell so far, they used Primacord on the outside of the hull. The stuff burns so fast that it cut off the hull at the waterline."

"Isn't that a lot of trouble just to sink a boat?""

"No question."

"Then why would they do it?"

"Maybe to make it go down real fast, or maybe to protect something inside from the direct blast. Like the body, maybe. They wanted the body to be found."

Rob walked toward the bow of the boat, examining each piece, hoping to find something with lettering on it from the bow, but the pieces that should have carried it, did not.

"If it was done on purpose, why aren't the state cops interested?" Rob asked.

"Because they don't know all the facts yet." He pointed to the middle sections. "I need to find more pieces. I've already sent several boards to be analyzed so I'll know what kind of explosive was used. Then I'll file a report. I think that may get them stirred up, and the ATF and FBI too."

Rob looked out through the windows in the back of the building, glancing absently across the harbor and then his jaw dropped, and he stood staring at a sleek, sixty-foot Cigarette boat just turning into the cut outside the harbor. "Chief!" He turned quickly. "Do you know who owns that boat?"

Chief Platt joined him at the window, looking at the boat, and wondering at the urgency in Rob's voice.

"Never saw it before."

"I got another story for you," Rob said and he told Chief Platt what he and Tom had seen, and about how the boat had chased them. They watched a tall, heavy set man walk to the stern as the boat circled and made ready to tie up at the fuel pier. The man turned slowly, looking around the harbor, examining each boat carefully. It didn't take long because most of the slips were still empty.

"I'll bet they're trying to find out who owns the boat they chased." Chief Platt slipped a cell phone from his jacket pocket and dialed the number for the store.

"Hi, is this Warren? Warren, this is Chief Platt. There's a boat just coming in to your fuel pier. If they start asking questions about who owns the English's boat, don't tell him anything. Just say you're new and you don't know. Good."

He turned and ran toward the front of the building, Rob following. "You stay here," he said. "There's a chance they might recognize you. I'm gonna pick off the hull numbers."

He ran outside, jumped into the truck, and drove out the pier toward the end. Rob watched from the back windows.

Chief Platt stayed in the truck, hidden by the tinted windows. He could see a guy on the Cigarette boat, scanning the harbor with his glasses. From where they had tied up they couldn't see the English's boat because it was tucked way back in the harbor behind the *Dottie E.*

Minutes later the big man came out of the store and walked down the pier to his boat. He climbed aboard easily, and two crewman hauled in the lines as another put the helm over, and started out of the harbor. One of them was watching the truck on the other pier as Chief Platt got out, pulled something from the back of the truck, and walked down the gangway to the lower dock out of sight.

The big boat idled along, slipping into the cut between the two stone jetties, and then violated the no-wake limit, as the helmsman pushed the throttles hard forward and with a huge roar the boat shot out into the open water, swung toward Woods Hole, and in seconds was just a dot fading into the horizon, the wake trailing out behind.

Rob walked back to the front of the building. He was standing by the door when Chief Platt returned.

"Did you get the numbers?"

"There were none that I could see. They may have been on the starboard side, but I don't think so."

"What do we do next?"

Chief Platt grinned. "What I do is one thing, what you do is another. Now look, Rob, I know guys your age see things like this as a terrific adventure, but you need to get that idea out of your head. I don't know what's going on here, but I can tell you, it's pretty serious."

"You think they're connected?"

"I know they are."

"Wow!"

"Now listen to me, okay?"

Rob nodded.

"You're out of this. You don't know anything. Don't talk to anyone about it."

"Everybody already knows that I found the body. And Tom was with me when they chased us. And there's also the girl who was on the beach with me when we found the body."

"Tell them not to talk about it to anyone."

"Can you tell me what's going on?"

"No. For your own good. You saw the body, right?"

"Yeah."

"You saw the face, right?"

He nodded.

"That's a trademark. I saw it down in Florida three years ago. That's all I'm gonna tell you, because in this case what you don't know may not hurt you."

"Don't you think I should tell my Dad and Carl, in case they want to take the boat out?"

"I'll call them, okay?" He looked down and then up quickly. "And don't take the boat out again until I say so. They'll be looking for you." He glanced away and then back as he sighed softly. "Rob, I can't tell you how dangerous this is. If you doubt me, remember that face. They kill anyone who gets in their way. Most of the time their victims just disappear. They left this one behind to warn someone; most likely someone on the Island, someone they're beginning to worry about."

"That fits," Rob said.

"Why?"

"Because I'm pretty sure the guy I found is Josh Warner from Oak Bluffs. He's the only guy I know who wore a belt like that. He hung around Wilson's Garage most of the time."

"What's Wilson's Garage?"

"That's where the drugs come from. I can't believe they haven't been busted. Every kid on the Island knows about it."

"Now you can see why you can't talk about this. Where is the girl now?"

"She goes to school in Connecticut."

"Tell her what I told you, but don't tell her anything else."

"Okay. I understand. In fact, you got me pretty scared here."

"Good. Stay that way."

"I'll just think about baseball."

"My son Bobby tells me you've got a major league fastball."

Rob looked blank for a second. "Bobby's your son? I didn't know that. He's gonna be a pretty darn good shortstop."

Chief Platt grinned. "Well, he made the team and Mr. Harden told him he can expect to get some playing time, so that's a good start." He laughed. "He says he just hopes he doesn't have to face you again in batting practice."

Rob grinned. "Tell him I only throw it over the plate."

"So I hear. At around ninety miles an hour."

Rob shrugged. "I just hope I can keep it up. I guess I'll find out Tuesday."

"I'll be there," Chief Platt said. "From what I hear the whole Island will be there."

Rob shook his head. "I always thought it would be cool being famous, but I'm beginning to have second thoughts."

"Just play ball and forget this. It's what I was sent here for."

"Really? You were sent here?"

"We had a tip three years ago. I did a lot of smuggler interdiction in Florida. Now, that's enough information. Get out of here, think about pitching, and say nothing!"

Rob grinned. "It's okay, Chief," he said. "I got the message."

But as he drove home, he wondered if he had. It was pretty hard to forget about something like this. In fact, it was impossible. He thought about the face again, smashed beyond recognition, the eyes missing. Had they done that before they killed him? And now he wondered if the guys on the Cigarette boat had gotten a look at them. Neither he nor Tom had thought to hide their faces. He didn't think he'd ever had a scarier thought.

Poor Josh. What had he gotten himself into? It had to have had something to do with drugs, because if ever there was a pothead it was Josh. He was stoned most of the time. Some days he couldn't even pump gas and get it right.

The next thought sent a major league shiver up his spine. It was probably something Josh had seen that he wasn't supposed to, a deal going down, or maybe something worse. And now he and Tom were on the list of people who might have seen something they shouldn't have.

10

Stepping Up

He was so nervous he was sure he was gonna piss his pants. Not even Tom's bad jokes worked.

"So, what's this rumor I hear about you and Betty Hawkins, huh? Jeez, Rob, I know you're desperate, but a skank like that? Com'on on, man, guys like us, hotshot ballplayers, we got standards, you know?"

Rob sat hunkered down in front of his locker, his knees locked together, trapping his hands.

"You gonna be all right?" Tom asked

Rob shook his head. "I never felt like this."

"Even when you were throwing stones for money?"

"No. Never. All I can think about is screwing up with half the damn Island watching."

Tom looked up at the clock. "I never saw you so shook up. You'd think you were getting ready to ask Mandy Rivers out."

"Mandy?" It was a thought beyond thinking. Every guy in school wanted to go out with Mandy Rivers! She hadn't seen her shoes since she turned thirteen! He looked up, his eyes wide with disbelief. All the guys wanted to go out with Mandy. Except him. He wanted to go out with Mallory. But to date a girl like that, he needed to be a star, and right now he was a long, long way from that. But at least she wasn't here to watch. It was bad enough to fail in front of everyone he knew. He looked around at Tom. "Did you ever ask Mandy out?"

"Nope."

"How come?"

"Too scary, man."

"Why? I mean all she can say is no."

"Would you ask her out?"

Rob smiled again. "No, but not because I'm scared of her." Tom grinned and slapped him on the shoulder. "Hey, I heard about the girl who was with you on the beach when you found the body. Sly old Rob. Everybody thinks he's scared of girls and there he is working the summer crowd."

"She just happened to be there, that's all."

"Yeah, sure, Rob, and Michael Jordan can't jump, right?" He glanced at the clock, hearing the clatter of spikes as the rest of the team headed out to the field. "You ready?"

Rob's eyes widened. "Ready ... I think."

"Look, it's no big thing. Once you get out there and you get warmed up, you'll be okay, take my word for it. You'll be okay."

And for a while, warming up, his stomach settled, and he was pretty sure he could keep his pants dry, but his brain was still on fire. He tried to focus through it, concentrating on just throwing the ball to Tom, but there was nothing natural or easy about his motion. He was aiming the ball instead of throwing it, and he kept thinking about all the details that went into each pitch, wondering if his arm angle was right, or whether he was taking too long a stride ... there were so many things that could go wrong! How had he gotten himself into this? How had he imagined that he could just walk out there and throw strikes? It was nuts! It was just plain totally nuts!

Tom walked toward him. "Okay, ole buddy, this is it."

Rob nodded and walked over to Mr. Harden.

He smiled. "You look a little pale," he said. "You okay?"

"Sure," Rob said.

Mr. Harden placed a brand new ball in his hand. "Then go show 'em what you got!"

He walked slowly out to the mound, now, for the first time, fully aware of how many people there were. He could hear them mumbling to each other, and now and then there was a shout. "Go for it, Rob!" or, "Go get 'em Rob!"

He put his foot on the rubber and looked down at Tom, squatted behind the plate. All I have to do is throw. But when he went into his motion he felt as if his arms and legs weren't talking to each other. Somehow he got through the final warm ups without throwing it to the backstop, then he turned, and as he took the throw from Chris Hooper at third, he looked up.

Not only were the stands full but there were people sitting on the grass, and his stomach felt very empty. Why would so many people turn out to see a high school game? He took the throw and looked toward home.

"Batter up!" the ump called.

He didn't look at the batter, focusing only on Tom's mitt. They only had one signal, because he only had one pitch, and he rocked back into his motion and let it fly. The ball came in like a rocket, high, rising, and sliding to the outside. Strike or not, the sheer speed of it unnerved the batter.

"Ball one," the ump called.

He looked down at the ball, wondering what he'd done to make it slide that way. Was he throwing harder? Only one way to find out. He rocked back into his motion, his right foot rising in a high kick, his left leg driving his body forward.

"Ball two."

Again the ball had drifted to the left. Damn! He was throwing way too hard. And he wasn't taking enough time between pitches. Each time he got the ball back he started into his windup. It was almost as if he didn't want to be out there, and the best way not to be out there was to get it over with.

"Ball three."

The crowd had grown quiet, and he thought maybe he'd piss his pants after all. In the back of his mind, at some thin edge of conscious thought, he wondered how he could get this next pitch under control. How could he make it slide left and rise, without slipping out of the strike zone? Into the motion, feeling his body stiff and robot-like, he wound up, and threw.

"Take your base," the ump said.

Damn! He'd never walked anybody before, in fact he had never considered the possibility! This was getting weird. He looked up at Tom as he walked the ball out to the mound.

"Hey, Rob. Stay cool. Just throw."

He nodded, picked up the resin bag, dusted his hand, and dropped the bag onto the back side of the mound, telling himself that all he had to do was get one pitch over and he'd find the groove. But now, with a runner on, he had to pitch out of the stretch, and he wasn't used to that.

He stood with his right arm facing the plate, the side of his left foot against the rubber. As he reached up over his head with the ball hidden in the glove, he looked at the runner taking a one step lead from first, and then he turned toward the plate and pushed off with his left foot.

"Ball one."

Yeah, sure. Get one over. Some big-time pitcher he was....

"Ball two."

Okay, calm down. He looked down at the ball in his glove and then took his grip. A four-seam fastball. Nothing to it. He started his motion, watching the runner, thinking that if the guy took one more step he could pick him off. That he'd never tried a pick-off before didn't matter. He'd seen it on TV and he knew how to do it without balking. He had to keep his right foot from crossing behind his left leg. If it crossed he had to throw home. If it didn't, he could throw to first. He held the ball in close, waiting, stretching, pausing when he brought the ball back down to his chest, and then the runner took another step toward second, and he whipped a strike to Ian McGivern at first. The runner dove back to first right into Ian's tag.

The crowd roared its approval as his teammates whipped

the ball around the infield. He took the throw from Chris, and stepped back up onto the mound. It felt too high, as if they had made it especially high so everybody could see him screw up.

He rocked back, took his kick, and drove his left leg into the throw. It was a hummer, a blur, but it was inside off the plate, and the batter jumped back.

"Ball three."

Rob stepped back up onto the mound, ready to throw, but the batter wasn't too eager to get back into the box. Fast was one thing, but fast and inside was terrifying.

"Let's go, batter," the ump said, and the kid stepped in, but he didn't dig in with his spikes because he was more concerned with getting out of the way than using his bat.

This time the ball went low.

"Ball four, take your base."

Sweat, a cold, clammy sweat that felt like tiny streams of ice water, ran down his sides. He went into his stretch and peered over his shoulder at the runner. No pick-off this time. The guy wasn't more than a foot from the bag.

When he walked the next guy, he'd thrown twelve balls in a row, and that brought Mr. Harden out to talk with him.

"You feeling okay, Rob?"

"Sure, Coach."

"You arm's okay?"

"It's fine."

"A little nervous maybe?"

Rob shrugged. "Yeah, I guess so. I feel kind of disconnected."

"I can see your timing's off," Mr. Harden said. "It's pretty normal to feel this way the first time. Just throw the ball. I'm not gonna take you out. I don't care if you walk the whole team."

Rob grinned. "I'm doing a pretty good job so far," he said.

Mr. Harden grinned back at him. "That was one heck of a pick-off move you made. Where'd you learn to do that?"

"Watching television."

"I gotta tell you, Rob, there's not many guys in the majors who have a move like that."

"They're staying pretty close to the bag now."

"Let me ask you something. Suppose you threw a little slower? You think these guys can catch up to you?"

"I never thought about it."

"Well, it's something anyway."

"Awful lot of people," he said.

Again Mr. Harden grinned. "Get used to it, my friend."

"Hey, Coach! You ready?" the ump called.

Mr. Harden slapped Rob on the butt. "Go get 'em!"

But instead he walked the next batter and loaded the bases. He stepped off the mound, picked up the resin bag and tossed it in his hand, dropped it, and looked around. He spotted his mother and father and his brother sitting together, and then he spotted Hal and ... damn! There was Mallory sitting right next to him! His stomach rolled over, and he had to swallow hard to keep from puking. What the heck was she doing here?

He looked back toward his family and he saw Carl toss a

pure white piece of quartz into the air and catch it. It was exactly the kind of stone he liked best for throwing. It was smooth and almost round and ... he grinned as he looked down at his feet and shook his head. That's all it was. Just breaking' stones, nothing more. Just breakin' stones. He stepped up onto the mound, watching the batter stand in. Then he focused on Tom's glove and started his windup. Nothing to it. Just another stone.

"Strike one!" the ump called as the ball smacked into Tom's mitt, and the crowd roared.

Betcha five bucks you can't do it again!

"Strike two!"

Make it ten and you're on!

"Strike three!"

The team had come alive behind him, shouting now, hollering encouragement, and the noise from the people in the stands felt electric. He could feel the energy, and suddenly he understood what it meant to play at home. They're on my side, he said to himself. They want me to win.

It was like looking down a pipeline to the plate. Once he started his motion there was nothing but a hole in the air, and he threw the ball through the hole and into the pipe. And now he was throwing harder, pumped by the energy he gathered from the crowd. He started his pitch a little low and watched it rise up into the strike zone. He started it on the inside of the plate and watched it slide to the outside corner. He tried it over and over and discovered he could control not just the center of the plate, but the corners, and that was what every pitcher wanted. It was even easier than breaking stones.

The smack of the ball in Tom's mitt echoed over the field, and the effect on the visiting team was clear. The last batter of the inning stood so far from the plate he couldn't have reached it with his bat. He didn't even want to. It would hurt too much, if by some chance he happened to connect.

Rob sat down on the bench and slipped his jacket over his shoulder, hoping his guys would get him some runs, but also hoping they'd make it fast because now he wanted to get back out there before the magic faded.

In the third inning Tom singled, and stole second. Ian singled him home and then Pete Pinkham hit a major shot over the center field fence. That gave him a three to nothing lead. All he had to do was throw strikes. The first inning was only a bad memory now, and pitch after pitch came in over the plate, just below the letters. High heat! He was throwing high heat! Nobody even fouled a pitch off. They simply couldn't catch up.

In the first inning he'd faced six men and not given up a run. After that he faced only three men an inning and every ball he threw was a strike. And then with the crowd roaring, the last batter came up to the plate. The noise was almost deafening. For a second, he thought about trying a change-up, and then he caught himself. Cocky! You start thinking cocky and you go away from what you know how to do. He cranked into his motion and let it fly. Two pitches later the game was over and people were screaming and running all over the place. His teammates kept pounding on his back and jumping into the air as he strolled to the bench, took off his glove, and slipped into his jacket. A no-hitter! His first game and it was a no-hitter! Unbelievable!

Carl got there first, grabbed him by both shoulders and hugged him once hard and stepped back. "Kind of a wobbly start there, Little Brother," he said.

Rob grinned. "You saved me, Carl."

Carl reached out. "Here," he said. "You might want to keep this in your pocket."

Rob looked down at the stone in his hand, grinned and tucked it into his pocket. "I'm gonna need it," he said.

"Not for long, Little Brother, not for long."

His folks came up and then Hal and Mallory, and she threw her arms around him and kissed him and then stepped back. "Rob," she said, "that was unbelievable!" She turned to her father. "Wasn't it, Dad?"

Hal grinned and shook his head. "I've been watching baseball a long time, Rob, and I never saw anything like that."

He grinned and hugged his mother.

"Well, whattya think of that?" George English said. "Wasn't that just something!"

"I don't think he's gonna be a carpenter, George," Hal said.

"Not a chance. Couldn't make a square cut if his life depended on it." He turned and introduced Mallory to his family.

Rob couldn't take his eyes off her, and he couldn't think of anything to say.

"God, Rob," Mal said. "That really was incredible!"

He smiled and blushed, wondering if he'd ever blushed in his entire life. "Thanks," he said.

"Listen," his dad said, "we're ordering in pizza for a celebration." He turned to Mal and her father. "Why don't you get Mrs. Farrow and come over to the house?"

"We'd love to," Hal said. He held up a video camera. "We can even watch the highlights." He lowered the camera. "Can you give us about an hour?"

"That'd be just perfect. Now Rob, you go get that arm taken care of," George said. "We'll meet back at the house."

He smiled at Mallory, his heart rate quickening as she smiled back. What a day! What an impossible day! Could it possibly get any sweeter? If it didn't, who cared? "See you later," he said, then turned and trotted toward the locker room, wondering if he had even been alive until now.

The pizza disappeared quickly and then they sat back in their chairs, the conversation drifting from questions to answers as each family learned more about the other. In a lull, when no one could think of anything to say, Hal spoke up. "Rob," he asked, "how did you get out of that first inning?"

Rob reached into his pocket and pulled out the stone Carl had given him. It was a sea-polished lump of quartz the size of a walnut and he held it out for all to see. "I looked into the stands and Carl was tossing it up and down. I didn't know what I was doing wrong until I saw the stone."

"We all need a talisman from time to time," Hal said.

"I never thought things like that worked," Rob said. "Now I think I just needed to concentrate on what I knew."

"Like finding your way in the dark," Hal said.

Rob nodded. "You mean by not looking in the direction you want to go? Sometimes I see best when I'm not looking."

George and Linda looked wide-eyed at their youngest son, wondering where this was coming from.

Rob grinned at them. "I read a lot, remember?"

Carl laughed. "My absolutely amazing, not-so-little-anymore brother. All this hidden stuff! Just like Grandpa Whitmore, always taking people by surprise."

He blushed again. It was getting to be an annoying habit. Still, it was an interesting comparison, because Grandpa Whitmore was not only the tallest member of the family at six-four, but he was always reading something. The house was filled with books. Not the usual way for a boat builder.

"How did you get along with Walt Connor?" Hal asked.

"He was great," Rob said. "He laid out a full program for me and I'm following it just the way he told me. It was really nice of you to do that, Hal. Thanks again."

"No thanks needed."

What he wanted to do was take a walk with Mallory, but he couldn't see how that would work, and then Carley Farrow made it all possible. "Why don't I give you a hand with this mess, Linda?" she said.

Linda English smiled. "Thanks, Carley."

"What are you working on these days?" Hal asked.

George and Carl brightened immediately. "Come on, I'll show you. We're doing a set of cabinets. Very fancy, curly maple edged with ebony. Handsome! Absolutely handsome! Had to ask him to put something down so I could buy the lumber. Got the maple over in Connecticut, got the ebony in Boston."

Rob leaned toward Mallory. "Want to take a walk?"

"Of course," she said. "Where do you want to go?"

"Lucy Vincent?"

"Sure." She stood up. "Mom, we're going down to Lucy Vincent for awhile."

"How long will you be?"

"An hour?"

"That's fine, Mal."

They rode in the Jeep, down Middle Road, talking as easily as if they'd known each other for years.

"What did they find out about the body?" Mallory asked.

"The state cops handle all the big crimes, and they aren't telling anybody anything."

"Maybe they don't know anything yet."

"Maybe."

"What do you think is going on?"

"I think it's probably drug smugglers or something. Chief Platt says he saw the same thing in Florida."

"The same what?"

"The way the guy was killed. It was pretty ugly."

"Like what?"

"They smashed his face to pieces and pulled out his eyeballs. It's their trademark. They do it to warn other people off."

"God, that is truly gross." She shook her head. "Ugh!"

"That's why I didn't want you to look," he said.

"I'm glad I didn't. Just hearing about it is almost too much."

"Chief Platt told me not to talk about it to anyone, and he wants you to do the same."

"Is it really so dangerous?"

"That's what he says." It was hard not to tell her about being chased and the other boat blowing up, but the less she knew the better. "How did you get out of school?"

"Daddy told them I had to do something with the family. They can't say anything. I'm a senior and I've already been accepted at college, so spring semester doesn't really mean much."

"I never get out of school," Rob said, sounding just the least bit put upon, but then he laughed. "On the other hand, I kind of like school these days. In fact I wouldn't miss it. For three-and-a-half years I was a ghost, and now everybody talks to me."

"Especially the girls, right?"

"Yeah, they do," he said, sounding surprised.

They turned left at Beetlebung Corner and headed out South Road toward the turn to Lucy Vincent Beach.

Rob parked the Jeep, and they climbed out, and started walking toward the water. The night was mild, and with the wind from the north, the beach was in the lee, and a fat half moon hung just above the eastern horizon. Without a word, he reached for her hand, and she locked her fingers through his. He wondered if he would ever in his life have such a day as this. Ahead of them the fine sandy ocean beach stretched in a long gentle curve toward a rocky point.

"How's your head doing?" she asked.

"What?"

"Your head. Will your hat fit when you put it on for practice tomorrow?"

He laughed. "Boy, you do get right to the point, don't you?"

"Like my father."

"He's a great guy."

"We're pretty lucky. Not only do we have parents, but we've got great parents."

"Now there's something I never much thought about."

"Sometimes, at school, I think I'm the only person who has both parents still at home. It isn't true, of course, but it seems like it. What's it like out here?"

"I don't know. I mean, the guys I know all have families, and so do the girls. But then I don't know a whole lot of kids very well. And there have been a lot of divorces."

"That's so hard to believe."

"What?"

"I mean, well, right from the first, on the beach, you seemed to be in control, I mean you didn't get rattled the way some guys do. So it stands to reason you ought to have a lot of friends."

"I was a dwarf, remember. Nobody included me in anything. I was like a boat that couldn't find its way to shore."

"Rob, that's so sad. It must have been terrible."

"I guess I didn't have much fun, and I know I resented it,

but I didn't spend a lot of time worrying about it." He smiled. "Do you know a writer named Philip Craig?"

"No."

"He writes mysteries set on the Vineyard. They're really good, but anyway, his main character, J.W. Jackson, has a sign over his kitchen door that says, 'No Sniveling.' When Dad read that he went right out to the shop, made a sign, and hung it over the door to the kitchen."

"I saw it!"

"It pissed me off, at first, but every time I started whining about my miserable fate, someone would point to the sign. Pretty soon I stopped whining and just started doing stuff on my own. That's when I started fly fishing and Carl finally took me duck hunting, and last year I got my first deer. Nobody in the world has an older brother like Carl. Just like Dad, he's patient, and they're always teaching me stuff. Even Mom does that. She's teaching me how to cook and sew and how to keep the books for the business. And I spent a lot of time reading. The only thing I watched on television were movies and baseball. In those books I found out what my parents were up to. I had to learn to live with what life handed me." He looked out across the water, his eyes following the silver path to the moon.

"And then you started to grow."

"Yeah." He shook his head. "It'll be hard not forgetting what I learned. No matter what, I have to remember that."

"Have you done anything about college?"

"I talked to my guidance counselor. I'll take the SATs in a

125

month or so and she gave me a bunch of catalogs. Mr. Harden, my coach, said that if after three or four games I still look as good as I do now, he'll call some college coaches he knows. He says those guys can always get you into school." He grinned at her. "That was really nice today, when you kissed me. Nobody ever did that before."

"Nobody ever kissed you?"

"I mean a girl."

"What else?"

"It's just that nobody ever did."

"I'm kind of impulsive sometimes."

"Doesn't get in *my* way," Rob said.

"I really didn't know what was going on 'til Daddy explained it. He said what you did today might happen once in a million times."

"Really? He said that?"

"He's also looking forward to going fishing. In fact he's so pumped that whenever he talks about it, he starts pacing around like a lion in a cage. Fathers want sons, and he got girls."

He stopped and turned her toward him. "That's just because men and boys do the same stuff. But he taught you how to fish, and don't you think he's hoping you'll go fishing with him?"

"I shouldn't have said that, I guess, but sometimes, I just, well you know...."

"Hey! No sniveling!"

She laughed and then pulled away from him and began

walking again. "You're right! No sniveling."

"And besides, the only reason you can't go with us is because you're away at school. As soon as you're home, you're going." He took her hand again. "Of course you'll have to get up before dawn, but that's a small price to pay."

"It is not! I need my beauty rest."

"Why? It couldn't make you any prettier."

That was when she kissed him a second time.

Later, when the house was quiet he lay in bed, staring up at the ceiling, trying to fall asleep and not having much luck. He wasn't even sure he wanted to sleep. His life had suddenly become something he had dreamed about but had never expected would go beyond the dream.

That left his brain whirling, unable to stay with a single thought for more than a few seconds. And it kept leaping ahead as if it were trying to create a new dream, as if it were trying to reach out into the future.

Each time he pulled it back to reality and then immediately let it graze among a new and absolutely fantastic set of possibilities. It wasn't something he hadn't done before but now ... now even the most improbable ideas seemed probable, the most impossible dreams, reachable.

Already the misery of his life up till now had begun to fade. It was like being aboard a boat as it disappeared into a fog bank. He was leaving things behind and all he had to do to navigate

safely through the fog was to keep his eye on the compass because only the compass provided any connection with the real
world. Even so, you could never be certain where you'd be when
you came out of the fog.

How many times had he been out in the boat and come in
through the fog, thinking he was dead on for the harbor, only
to find himself a mile or so one way or the other.

He shook his head and rolled onto his side and then suddenly sat up in bed and listened, holding his breath. A second
later he pulled on his jeans and a tee shirt and his boat shoes and
headed downstairs in the dark.

He opened the gun case and took out his shotgun, slipped
a shell into the receiver, ran it closed and loaded two more into
the magazine. He knew what he'd heard. The rattle of the door
latch on the shop.

Slowly, he eased out through the back door into the night.
The moon had dropped low into the western sky but it still
threw plenty of light and he moved to the corner of the house
and looked down toward the shop.

The door was open and he waited, trying to decide whether
to sneak up, throw on the lights and confront whoever it was,
or whether to slip back inside and wake Dad and Carl. He re-
coiled back as the lights in the shop went on and then he heard
the radio start. What kind of a burglar turned the radio on?
How crazy was that?

And suddenly he heard the voice of Johnny Cash. It was

the tape that Dad always played when he was working, sometimes humming along, sometimes whistling and that was what he heard next, Dad's soft whistle.

He lowered the gun, unloaded it, and walked to the shop.

"Hey, Rob," his father said, "what are you doing up?"

"I couldn't sleep and I heard the latch on the door."

George grinned and pointed to the shotgun. "Maybe I oughta leave a note or something when I come out here at night."

"I never knew you did that?"

"All the time. Get an idea and I can't sleep till I get something down on paper. Got to see it. Got to make it real before I know whether it'll work."

Rob leaned the gun against the wall and sat on a stool by the work bench.

"That was really something today, Rob."

"It hasn't really sunk in yet.."

"Wouldn't expect it to. Things like that take a while. Then you do it again and then again and suddenly it's just a matter of the way things are supposed to be."

"You think I can do it again?"

George laughed. "No question. And Hal and Carl agree with me. That was no accident.."

"Would it be too weird to say that it felt right?"

"Nope. Sometimes things just feel that way. It's how you know where to go next."

11

Hanging Out

Working out had become a religion. First the weights, then a two-mile run, and, as usual, some off-day throwing; warm up tosses, and then fifty pitches at medium speed. On school days he spent the first part of practice in the weight room, then on the road, and finally on the field. On Saturdays, he got the first part done and then Tom showed up for the throwing.

He came in from running, carrying the mail, and smiling from ear-to-ear. There was a letter from Mallory and he took it up to his room where he could read it without interruption. He sat in the easy chair by the window that looked south toward the water. Now, with the leaves off the trees, he could see the distant glint of the Atlantic. He opened the letter and began to read.

> *Dear Rob,*
>
> *I meant to tell you about this after the game but somehow I didn't. I'm not even sure how to say this because I don't want you to get the wrong idea. I am going out with a guy here at Pomfret that I've been seeing since last year.*

We nearly broke up last summer, but we didn't. All my friends tell me that it won't last once we go off to different colleges (he's going to Stanford because he comes from California) and I'm going to Bowdoin, as I told you, and that's a long way apart. But for now we're still going out, and because of what happened on Tuesday, I wanted you to know about this. I told you I'm impulsive sometimes, but I like you a lot, Rob, a whole lot, and I wanted you to know that too.

I feel really awful about telling you this way, Please forgive me for writing like this. I hope you don't hate me.

Always,
Mallory

He set the letter in his lap and looked off toward the ocean, feeling an ache in his chest he had never felt, not even at the worst of times. He'd let himself hope, something he had learned not to do. Just take what comes and make the best of it. Work toward what you can, and the rest will take care of itself.

But this had been different. It wasn't something you could work at. It was either there or it wasn't, and now he knew that it wasn't. He could live with it because there wasn't any choice but to live with it. But why tell him in a letter? That sucked! Don't hate me ... right! What was he supposed to do, just go on being jolly old Rob the human doormat? Not a chance!

He crumpled up the letter and dropped it into his waste-basket as he headed downstairs. He had other fish to fry. It was time for his stretching exercises. He stopped halfway down the stairs, went back up to his room, pulled a book from the shelf and carried it out to the Jeep. At the post office he bought an envelope, addressed it, and dropped the book inside.

The clerk weighed it, he paid, and left. Never in his life, except when it came to deciding where to fish, had he followed an impulse so completely. And if it was wrong, if it backfired, so what? He sure wouldn't be any worse off than he was now.

After supper, he and Tom headed for Oak Bluffs to take in a movie and then go for pizza, something they had done for what seemed like all his life, though that was only because nobody's life started until they got their driver's license. What happened before that was the stuff your parents remembered.

But now things had changed again. Tom still found it hard to accept this new guy driving Rob's old Jeep Wrangler. In fact, he had discovered he was even a little in awe of this tall, rangy guy who could throw a baseball so effortlessly and so well. It had all happened so fast. And yet he didn't think Rob had changed much. He had never talked a lot, most times he just listened. He'd been like a ghost. Tom wondered how well anyone knew Rob English. If you asked them about him, what would they say? Would there be anything about his past, or would it all start with baseball? It was happening to him too. Like now. Suddenly he couldn't think of anything to talk about except baseball. Without warning another subject arose and he let it fly.

"Hey, Robster, tell me, really, how come you never said anything about finding a body on the beach?"

"I'm really sorry about that, Tom. I meant to and then I forgot," Rob said.

"Forgot! How could you forget something like that?"

"All I've had on my mind for the past two weeks is pitching." He reached into his left-hand jacket pocket and pulled out a baseball. "I carry this around with me all the time."

Tom laughed. "You're kidding, right? You carry a ball around? Man, talk about getting into it."

Rob rolled the ball in his hand until he had the stitches lined up for a four-seamer. "A guy my dad built a house for, Mr. Farrow, got a pitching coach to come up from New York and lay out a program for me. I do that every day."

"Whoa. A trainer from New York?"

"Mr. Farrow's part owner of the Pittsfield Mets and he got a guy from the organization to come up."

"Wait a minute! You're telling me that you worked out with a pitching coach from the Mets? Hey look, Rob, breakin' my stones is one thing, but this is just too much, okay?"

"Hey, would I lie to you? It's the truth. He flew up and spent a whole day with me."

"And you never told me? I thought we were friends...."

"That's got nothing to do with it. Didn't your mother leave the messages? I called about five times, and you were always out with Melissa. You never called back so I thought you were pissed about something."

"Naw, you're right. I guess I haven't been around much either." He pulled his cap down over his eyes. "Jesus! The Mets! I've been playing ball since I was six, you've been at it two weeks, and you've got a pitching coach from the Mets."

"It's not what you think," Rob said. "Mr. Farrow said a lot of young guys who can throw screw up their arm because nobody tells them how to throw or how to take care of their arm. He wanted me to do it right. That's all there is to it, Tom."

Tom charged ahead as if he hadn't heard Rob at all. "And another thing. After the game on Tuesday, we're standing around and suddenly this really hot girl comes out of nowhere and kisses you! Who is she?"

"Mr. Farrow's daughter Mallory. She goes to school off-Island." He let it go at that.

"Am I talking to the same guy here? I mean, like, the Rob English I know never played sports and he never, like ever, went out on a date."

"Girls want to look up at their dates, not down. And here's something else. I grew another inch this past month. I'm six-three! Can you believe it?"

"I think I'm getting a little jealous here."

"All right! Finally! Finally, someone's a little jealous of me! I spent my whole life being jealous."

Tom sat quietly for a while, thinking about what Rob had said. "I never thought about that. It must've sucked, huh?"

"Sometimes. Maybe even a lot of times. But what could I do? And anyway, I always had one good friend. You never laughed at me, and you always got pissed if someone else got on my case. What more could a guy ask for?"

"Rumor has it you've been seen hanging around the guidance office too."

"I'm gonna try to get into a college." He shrugged and then gripped the ball a little tighter. "I can't stay here."

"I'm cool with that. One day it's just time to go."

"As long as you have a place to go."

"You didn't take the SATs, did you?"

"I can take them next month."

"Tell me more about Mallory."

It was then he discovered that he didn't hate her and never would. Even more astonishing was knowing that he still hoped it could work out. "She's really nice. She's smart and...."

"Now wait a second here. Smart? Who says anything about a girl being smart? We're talking show here, Rob. I mean, like legs and hooters and...."

"Okay, I get your point, and I won't say I didn't think about all that, but most of all I like the way we get along with each other. I mean she talks to me like I'm a normal guy, you know?"

"What are you telling me? You're not normal?"

Rob laughed. "No. I'm telling you that I am now. And I know I am because that's the way Mallory talks to me."

"This could be serious. This is the way my brother started to talk before he got engaged."

"Engaged! Hey, we're talking friends here ... just friends."

"Yeah, right. Kisses mean something, you know."

Rob slipped the baseball back into his pocket. The car behind him was suddenly very close. He looked down at the speedometer. Forty. What was the guy trying to do? Pass him? Well, let him go! Rob pulled the Jeep over to the margin of the road, giving the guy plenty of room.

"Hey! Keep it on the road!" Tom shouted.

"There's a nutbag in a pickup on my bumper. I thought he wanted to pass."

Tom swiveled around and looked out the back of the Jeep. "Damn, he's really close, Rob."

Just then the truck leaped forward and rammed the back of the Jeep. Rob fought the wheel, keeping the Jeep straight as he steered away from the edge of the asphalt. "This guy is nuts!"

"Maybe you oughta try to outrun him!" Tom said.

Rob saw the truck start forward again and this time he stomped on the accelerator and when the truck hit, the jolt was not nearly so severe. Then he hit the brakes and the truck behind swerved and began to skid sideways as Rob stepped on the gas again and pulled away.

But it wasn't over, and the truck closed the distance rapidly, forcing Rob to speed up. For a mile or so the only time the truck closed was when Rob dropped below seventy.

"This is crazy!" Tom shouted. "Is he trying to kill us?"

Rob looked into the rearview mirror. No, he thought, he's not trying to kill us, he's trying to get us to kill ourselves. A short way ahead there was a sharp curve in the road. No way would they make it at this speed. "Hang on!" he shouted.

"What?"

"Hang on!"

Tom grabbed hold where he could and Rob hit the brakes. This time he kept them on and the driver of the truck hit his brakes, but he'd been a second too late and the truck went into a full skid, the tires screeching over the pavement as the truck slammed into the back of the Jeep just as Rob took his foot off the brake and shifted to neutral. The impact shot the Jeep forward, and he let it roll a ways before whipping the wheel around. The Jeep skidded in a slow arc to the right, coming around to face the truck. Then it stalled.

"Get out, Tom, run for it! Get into the woods! Fast!"

Tom threw open the door and dodged off between the close-growing trees. On his side Rob had a stone wall and a wide pasture and nowhere to hide. He started to get out of the Jeep when a big hand grabbed him and pulled him out.

He saw the punch coming and he ducked, and the guy's hand hit the metal bar under the soft top of the Jeep. He started swearing and hollering and shaking his arm. The only thing to do was run, and Rob dodged around the Jeep, keeping low, trying to get to the woods. A gun went off, and he heard the bullet whistle past him. The gun went off again, and this time the bullet flew through the windshield of the Jeep and came out through the plastic window in the back. Instinctively he looked toward the muzzle flash, and then ducked back behind the Jeep. He could see the guy, outlined by the lights of the truck. He was trapped.

"I broke my damn hand!" the first guy hollered.

"Never mind your hand! Circle around the Jeep and flush him out into the open!"

Rob reached into his pocket, grabbed hold of the baseball, and pulled it out.

"What am I supposed to do with a broken hand!"

"Just shut up and do as you're told!"

"I can't!"

Rob stepped back, keeping low, and while they were arguing he whipped the ball at the shooter, putting everything he had into it. The guy never saw it coming and it hit him in the side of his head, just behind the temple, with a sickening crack. He dropped to the ground without a word and the other guy turned and ran back toward the truck. "Hey, Billy! What the hell happened?"

Rob slipped into the woods and lay still.

"Damn, how did he do that?" the first man said, and then ran for the truck. He jumped in, backed it around, and tore off in the direction they had come.

Rob stepped back out of the woods and walked to the man he had hit. There was hardly any blood but there was a clear liquid oozing out of his skull. What did I do, here? Did I kill him? Jesus, I hope I didn't kill him! He turned and ran for the Jeep, pulling the cell phone out of the leather pouch on the dash. He was so nervous he could hardly dial.

His father and Carl got there before the police, and by then Tom had come back out of the woods. They stood looking at the body of the man lying in the road, awash in the lights from George's truck, trying to make sense out of what had happened.

"You hit him with a baseball?" George looked up at his son and shook his head. "Is it possible to throw a baseball that hard?"

"If Rob's throwing it," Carl said. "This was a lot closer than sixty feet too."

Rob pointed to the gun lying nearby. "Dad, the guy was shooting at me!" He pointed to the back of the Jeep. "Look at the Jeep. At least one round went right through it."

"But why would anyone be shooting at you, Rob? People just don't go around shooting at people without a reason."

"Twice they rammed into the back of the Jeep," Tom said.

"At first they weren't trying to kill us, Dad, they were trying to get us to go real fast. At one point I was going nearly eighty, but I could never have made the next curve at that speed, so I slammed on the brakes. I think they wanted us to run ourselves off the road."

It seemed as if they had hardly heard the sirens before the police descended from two of three possible directions. They came from Chilmark, and West Tisbury, and the state trooper from Vineyard Haven, Paul Bianca, showed up too. He'd been out of the Academy for a year and a half and on the Vineyard for six months. Worse, having grown up in Boston, he knew nothing about small towns, and with about twelve thousand people on a hundred and twenty-six square miles, the Vineyard is a small community ... at least in the off season.

What followed was a huge amount of confusion and several arguments between Al Bond, the Chilmark chief, and Paul Bianca, who wanted to take Rob down to Edgartown and hold him on suspicion of murder. But Al was having none of it.

"Jesus, Paul, where the hell do you think he's going?" Al adjusted his trousers upward against the dome of his stomach.

"That's not the point," Bianca shot back at him. "The point is, there's been a murder here!"

"Murder? This is no murder! This is self defense?"

"You know what I think I'm looking at here, Al? I think I'm looking at a simple case of road rage!"

Warren Bolt, the cop from West Tisbury, sided with Al. "Look, Paul, Rob's going nowhere. And besides, you heard what Tom said about the guy shooting at Rob, you can see the bullet holes in the Jeep, and you already picked up the gun."

Young, sleekly fit, and very much impressed by his own authority, Bianca was unconvinced. All he could see was an arrest for murder. He started to reach for his cuffs when George English stepped in front of him.

"What is this, anyway?" he asked. "You always arrest the last man standing? Is that it?"

"This is police business," Bianca said.

"No. We're talking about a young man who took down a gunslinger with a baseball in order to keep from getting shot. You put him in jail and you mark him for life, and I'm not having that."

"Are you interfering with an officer here, Mr. English? Is that what I'm hearing? Because if that's what I'm hearing...."

"No, sir." George kept his voice low and calm. "What you're hearing is a father asking you not to put the mark of Cain on his son. That's what I'm asking."

"Look, Mr. English, I got a job to do here."

"How long do you expect to be on this island?"

"Is that a threat?"

"Common sense. For most of the year everybody knows everybody. We may not get along always, but most of us will help when there's trouble. You throw Rob in jail and nobody will talk to you. Isn't that right, Al?"

"Probably is," Al said. "Pretty close-knit community. They trust you, you can get answers. They don't, and you'll get nothing." He hitched up his pants again. "You can call that a threat, but it's more like George says, common sense. You're from away. Remember, what happens during the summer has got little to do with what this place is like the rest of the year. You're in a small town now."

"Okay, you want to know what my problem with this is? Here's my problem. I don't believe a kid can throw a baseball hard enough to kill someone, okay? So I'm guessing that something else is going down here and until I find out what, I need to hold on to the only suspect."

"Maybe you should have watched the two games he's pitched," Carl said. "The Chilmark police used their radar gun, and they clocked one pitch at ninety-eight miles an hour. That was sixty feet from where he threw it. This is more like about thirty feet. Isn't that right, Al?"

Al nodded.

Tom walked over and held out his left hand. "I'm his catcher," he said. "Look at my hand."

Al shone his light on Tom's hand and they could all see how red and swollen it was. "I used two sponges inside my glove and the last time I caught him was yesterday."

Bianca looked over at Rob. "How tall are you?"

"Six-three," Rob said.

"How much do you weigh?"

"One-seventy-five."

"How old are you?"

"Eighteen."

"Okay. Maybe you're right," he said to Al. "You gotta understand that I'm taking a big risk here."

"I understand," Al said. "But, the truth is, Paul, if I thought Rob was likely to run off, I wouldn't argue with you. Nor would anyone else here. Not even his father. I've known Rob since he was born, we all know each other. If Rob tells you he hit the guy with a baseball, you can take it to the bank. What Tom says, you can add to the account. I'll tell you what really worries me, is why someone would attack these two guys. And look at the gun. That's no Saturday night special, Paul. It's a Glock nine-millimeter. From what I read in the newspapers a lot of bad guys carry guns like that."

Bianca nodded. "Okay. No arrest." He looked at Rob. "You've got a lot of people on your side. Don't let 'em down."

"I won't," Rob said. "And thanks. I told you the truth. But

maybe we need to sit down and talk because I think this might be connected to that body I found on the beach and a Cigarette boat that chased us back from Quicks Hole."

Bianca looked up quickly. "What boat?"

"Do you want me to tell you now?"

"No. I got enough to do here. I'll call you in the morning. Why don't you all go home? Al and Warren and I have a lot to get done before the coroner gets here."

Back at the house they all sat around the big table in the kitchen as Linda English set out cold cuts and bread, mayonnaise and mustard.

"I'm glad I'm not sitting in the Edgartown jail," Rob said. "I can't believe that guy!"

"He was doing what he thought was his job," George said.

"Guys like that give cops a bad name," Carl said.

"The other trooper there is a lot worse than Bianca," Tom said. "All he does is harass teenagers. He's not as bad as The Ultimate Onager, but he's pretty bad."

"Don't blame Bianca," George said. "Think what it would be like if you were in his shoes. Remember, he's got to write a report, and he's got a dead man to account for. Not easy. And, what's more important, he listened to Al when he should have listened. And after he'd listened, he changed his mind. My opinion is, we're lucky to have a young fella that smart."

Carl looked around at his father, his eyebrows arched in surprise. Then he nodded. Dad was right. No question.

"Maybe I shouldn't have thrown the ball so hard," Rob said.

"I didn't even think about what it might do. I mean, he was shooting at me, and I was trying to get away, and then he had me trapped behind the Jeep, and the other guy was getting ready to close in. It was the only thing I could do."

Carl grinned over at him. "You did it perfectly. If you hadn't taken him out, you'd be dead."

"I feel kind of weird," Rob said.

"When I was in Viet Nam," George said, "it took a lot to get used to killing people, but you did it, and you worried about it later, because if you didn't, you weren't around to worry about it later. Nobody liked it, at least the guys I knew, but there was no choice. But that was war, so it was easier to understand, and it was easier to live with."

"I could've hit him someplace else," Rob said.

"No, you couldn't have," Linda said. "Listen to your father, Rob. He's telling you about growing up. He was the same age you are now when he was in Viet Nam. It's always tough to have to grow up all at once."

"Hell," Carl said, "it's just tough to grow up."

Sirens In The Night

12

They were far enough from the fire station so that only on a southerly wind could they hear the siren. But both George and Carl were volunteers, so when the sirens went off, their beepers sounded, and they were never quiet about having to get up in the middle of the night.

Even so, Rob nearly slept through, and then suddenly he was awake, staring into the dark, his heart hammering. Without questioning what he was doing, he climbed out of bed, dressed as fast as he could, and ran downstairs.

"What are you doing up?" Carl asked.

"I'm going with you," Rob said.

Carl looked at him quizzically, scratched his head, and pulled his Red Sox cap over his blond hair. "That's up to Dad."

"I know." He walked into the pantry and came out with a box of Ritz crackers. "Want some?"

Carl grinned. "Do you ever stop eating?"

"Just a growing boy." He took a small block of cheddar cheese from the fridge and stuck it into his pocket.

Carl laughed. "Talk about an understatement."

"Okay!" George raced into the kitchen. "Let's go!"

"Can I go with you?" Rob asked.

George took a second to react, then nodded his head. "Always need more volunteers. But for now all you do is watch."

They rode three across in the pickup, the blue warning light flashing from the dashboard. Not that they needed it, because there was no traffic at all until they got to the fire station.

The pumper was just pulling out, heading west toward Menemsha, and they let the emergency truck follow, and then got in line. It took just minutes to reach Menemsha, and they could see the glow in the sky as they turned left toward the beach, and then left again, and up onto the road above the harbor.

But not until they climbed out did they see the fire.

"It's our boat!" Carl shouted. "Our boat's on fire!" He ran to the pumper and began pulling out the hose, running down between the cottages on the harbor, and when the water came on, he aimed it directly at the heart of the fire, trying to separate it from the wood. But it was way, way too late. George took the second hose and played it on the fire even as he made sure to wet down the fishing shacks and the other boats nearby.

Across the harbor, which at that point is only several hundred feet wide, the Coast Guard crew, using their high-pressure pumps, sprayed water on everything that might burn.

The fire was hot, too hot to be just the boat burning. Someone had set this, and they had probably used gasoline, Rob thought. The question was whether they would be able to get it out before it got to the fuel tanks, and now, because that same thought had occurred to everyone, every hose was turned on their boat. It was no longer a matter of saving the boat, but keeping it from exploding into a shower of burning rubble raining on the other boats, cottages, fish houses, and piers.

In the distance they could hear more sirens, and Rob guessed they had probably called for assistance from Aquinnah and West Tisbury. Diesel didn't go up the way gas did, but it would blow, and if the tanks got hot enough it would be hard to tell the difference. Just now that looked like a real possibility and .... damn ... Carl was way too close!

Rob ran down the embankment and grabbed his brother by the shoulder. The noise from the fire was almost deafening. "Carl!" he shouted. "Carl, you're too close!"

"I've got to stop it!" Carl shouted back.

Rob looked at the fire and then at his father who had drawn well back, far enough to escape the concussion from the blast. He did not know how he knew, he just knew. He grabbed Carl by the waist, and using all his strength, jerked him away from the hose, and out over the water.

The explosion let go just as they hit the surface of the water and went under. Not for long. The water was far too cold, and they popped up and grabbed onto the piles on the next pier.

"Jesus, Rob!"

"It was gonna go," Rob said.

"How did you know?"

They swam to the ladder on the pier and climbed up as two other volunteers tried to subdue the hose Carl had been using.

Left to itself, the hose was thrashing and dancing like an enormous snake as the men worked their way hand over hand up to the nozzle. Once they had the hose under control, they turned and began dousing the spot fires started by the falling rubble.

"Well, that's a first," Carl said. "Never been swimming this early before, and I'll tell you something. It's cold!"

Rob laughed, as much out of relief as anything. "You're right," he said. "That water is truly cold."

George met them as they walked off the pier. "Damn, that was close! Are you both okay?"

"I think so," Rob said, as he looked around at his brother.

"Only thanks to Rob," Carl said. And then he asked the question again. "How did you know? Better yet, what made you suddenly want to go to a fire?"

Rob shook his head. "Just a feeling," he said.

"Okay," Carl said. "A dumb question. All I know is you did, and I'm alive, and I haven't got a mark on me, and who knows what kind of shape I'd be in if you hadn't been here. You saved me, Little Brother, you flat-out saved my tail."

Rob grinned. "S'what brothers are for," he said, using the words Carl had so often used with him.

"You're really all right?" George asked again.

"Pretty cold," Rob said.

"Go get into the truck and get the heater going. You'll have pneumonia! Better yet, take the truck and go home and get into a hot tub. I'll call ahead so your mother's prepared. I'll get a ride home with someone."

Carl grabbed his brother by the arm. "What was I thinking of? You can't get sick now. Not even a stupid cold. You got a game on Tuesday!"

Linda was ready with hot chocolate and two bath tubs full of hot water by the time they got home.

"All right," she said as she handed them each a steaming mug of chocolate. "Both tubs are full and hot. Don't waste a second! Get up there and get warm. No quicker way to get sick than to let your body temperature drop."

By the time both her sons were dry and warm, George had arrived, and they all sat around the big oak table in the kitchen.

"You think the fire was set?" Carl asked his father.

"Of course it was set," George said. "No fire burns like that, without it was set."

"But why would anyone want to burn up our boat?"

"To keep me from nosing around," Rob said.

"But they must have figured that you told somebody what you saw," Carl said. "Maybe it was meant as a warning."

"What about the two men who tried to run Rob and Tom off the road?" Linda asked. "Was that just a warning too?"

They could hear the panicky edge in her voice.

"That was more than a warning," George said. "But maybe they hit the boat because there was no one there. After all, they lost one guy tonight, so maybe they decided to back off a little."

"I sure hope so," Carl said. "I don't much like having to look over my shoulder all the time."

149

"Well, don't stop now," George said. "Not until this is over." He stood up and walked to the gun case, unlocked it and took out two Colt .45, Government Model pistols. Then he slipped loaded clips into each one and brought them back to the table, handing one to Carl. "From now on, one of us goes with each of you. We're licensed to carry and that's what we're going to do."

"I don't like carrying guns," Linda said.

"Well, I don't like it much either," George said, "but there's no choice. This is a war and we've got to think like it's a war. Carl, you'll drive Rob to school and then go back in the afternoon for practice and drive him home. Linda, I'll stay with you."

Rob looked up at his father, surprised by how different he looked. There was a cold, hard light in his eyes, a light he had never seen before, and he thought he would not want to be on the other end of that forty-five. He could see it in Carl too. It would be a great fool who challenged either of them. They were both expert shots, as was he, and they practiced every week. It was a simple rule in the English household. You learned how to shoot because you never knew when you might have to defend yourself, and you simply couldn't count on having the cops there to help when you most needed them. And as Dad always said, it wasn't the cops' fault, it was just a matter of the time it took to get from wherever they were.

His mother could shoot too, and she even had her own gun. It was only a twenty-two Smith & Wesson, but she was very accurate and the clip carried ten rounds. The question, though, was whether she could pull the trigger, if it came to that. For that matter, could any one of them, except Dad, shoot another human being? Could he do that now, when he wasn't fighting in a war? On the other hand, was it so much different than what he'd done? Wasn't it just a matter of trying to save yourself or someone else? Had he intended to kill the guy with a baseball? How could you be sure about such a thing? Wasn't it more likely that when you aimed a gun at someone and pulled the trigger, you intended to kill them? But he was a good enough shot to shoot someone in the leg or the shoulder and disable them, or at least he thought he was. He wondered if you could ever know such a thing before it happened. One thing he knew. He didn't like being someone who had killed a man. What he did like, though, was knowing that he had faced a deadly test and he had passed, and he thought that would make him a much better man, if only because he knew what he could do when the time came. Right now, he only hoped it did not come again.

But how could they stop it? They didn't even know what was going on, or what he had done to cause two men to try to kill him. What they needed were answers. Then another thought occurred to him. "Does diesel fuel always go up like that?"

George looked at Carl and they both shook their heads. "No," George said. "There was a bomb on the boat, probably on a timer, set to go off about the time somebody got close."

Over the next few days nothing else happened except that he had to talk to some detectives from the State Police and they decided not to file charges. Nothing would appear on his record.

It had been, they said, self defense. An ATF agent showed up too, because they handle anything to do with bombs, but there wasn't much they could tell him.

On Tuesday, again in front of a couple of thousand people, Rob threw his third no-hitter, and they had now won five games without a loss.

On the same day, *The Vineyard Gazette* carried the story about what had happened on Saturday night and the next morning both the Boston Globe and the Cape Cod Times had the story. Then it got picked up by the wire services and the phone started ringing. The television people came down from Boston and interviewed him. Then *The Today Show* called and wanted him to go on, but he turned them down.

The blues were starting to run and he had games to pitch, and there was no way he could go all the way to New York. But more to the point, he wanted it all to simply go away. Fame sucked. At least this kind of fame, he thought. They never once asked him about his pitching and they never mentioned the team. They all seemed to think it was some kind of miracle that he could have thrown a baseball with such accuracy, and thrown it hard enough to kill a man. How could they be so dumb? Didn't they know why batters wore helmets?

Slowly, the phone stopped ringing, and by Friday it had stopped entirely, though he had not been forgotten. When he pitched on Friday, the stands were full of scouts and reporters.

For the first time he lost it, really lost it. He couldn't get his fastball over, and he had to cut down his speed so far that the other team began to hit the ball. Worse, the ump would not give him the corners. Pitch after pitch, he cut the black edge of the plate, and the ump wouldn't call a strike. He had to bring the ball into the center of the plate, and when he did they hit it.

He sat on the bench at the end of the fifth inning, his team trailing by two runs, trying to work out what had gone wrong. He considered whether his grip was right, whether he was taking too long a stride, whether his arm angle had changed in some way. What was he seeing? Was he focused on the target? And why the heck was life so full of questions you couldn't answer? Why wasn't it more like fishing where when you didn't catch anything it was most likely because the fish weren't there, or they simply weren't feeding.

He felt a hand on his shoulder and he turned to look at Hal.

"Kind of a rough day, huh?" Hal said.

"If I throw hard, I can't the ball over the plate," Rob said.

"It happens to the best pitchers," Hal said.

"What do they do?"

"Some never get it back. But you'll get it back, Rob. This is just a hiccup. I'm more interested in where you've decided to take me fishing in the morning."

"Sometimes, when the blues get here early, I've had good luck fishing Cape Pogue Gut. I thought we'd go there, and if that doesn't work we might try Wasque, but that's a tough place to work a fly rod. Most of the time you can't get out far enough. Usually I throw in some surf rods if I'm going out there. Do you mind fishing that way?"

"Fishing is fishing. I like it any way at all."

Rob grinned and looked toward the stands where he had seen the scouts before. Now they were gone. "Guess I didn't impress the scouts," he said.

"I wondered if you'd picked them out," Hal said.

"I wasn't sure at first, but they didn't look like they came from here."

Suddenly a roar broke from the crowd and they looked up to see the ball disappear over the left field fence as Tom started his home run trot. Two runners scored before him and now they were ahead by a run.

"Looks like you're back in the game," Hal said. He clapped him on the shoulder. "Tell your coach that from now on you only pitch with five days rest. Four days isn't enough. It isn't enough for most major leaguers, and it sure isn't enough for high school. How's your arm feel?"

"It's fine."

"Is it alive?"

"Yup."

"Good. What time will you pick me up?"

"Four. We need to catch the tide."

"Four it is."

Wally Wilson ended the inning with a long fly to right and Rob took off his jacket and walked back out to the mound. He felt no different as he took his warm-ups, and he was sure nothing had changed. There was something odd in his back pocket, and he stuck his hand into the pocket and there was the stone

Carl had given him. Damn! How could he have forgotten about that? He turned sideways and kicked the dirt away from the front side of the rubber, looking up as the first batter stepped in. When he let the first pitch go, he knew he was okay. The ball came in low and rose up into the strike zone, dead over the plate, and the batter swung but not until the ball had already smacked into Tom's glove.

A slow buzz passed over the crowd. The second pitch brought them to their feet as it cut the heart of the plate, and all he could think of was a line from some movie he couldn't even remember ... "I'm baaack...."

13

Flotsam, Jetsam, And Blues

In Carl's extended cab, four-wheel-drive pickup, they took the long way around, driving on the beaches out to Chappy, and then over the tarred road to the turn for Cape Pogue Gut. From there on the single-track road ran to sand and gravel. It was full daylight by the time they reached the water.

"The only trouble with fishing here," Carl said, "is having to lug the fish back uphill."

Hal laughed. "First we have to catch 'em."

"Oh, no need to worry about that. If Rob says there are fish someplace, you can be sure you're gonna catch fish. Half the guys on this island would like to know how he knows that. Last year during the Derby he had guys following him everywhere he went. He had to resort to pure skullduggery."

"I wore disguises," Rob said. "And I borrowed vehicles from other guys. It was almost as much fun as the fishing."

"What I want to know," Carl said, "is how come you win so many dailies and never win the big prize?"

Rob shrugged. "I know where the fish are. How big they are is another question."

"Even when he does things backwards, they work out." Carl tied a fly to the end of his line. "Like now. I've never fished here on an outgoing tide, but Rob says this is the place, so I'll do it, even if I think it's pretty weird."

"Jeez, Carl. Plenty of times I get skunked."

"Okay," Carl said. "Why here? Why on this tide?"

"Water temperature. We've had four sunny days in a row, the Pond is shallow, so the bottom warms up and that warms the incoming water. Not much, but just a couple of degrees, and that makes it almost perfect for blues at this time of year ... or at least it should."

They spread out along the shore. It was a difficult place to fish with a fly rod, because the high bank came up close to the channel, limiting the backcast. But they didn't have to cast more than thirty feet, and though even that distance would have tested most fly fishermen, it did not test them. They were far too practiced, even roll-casting the big flies, which ought to have been impossible, and would have been in any wind.

But the morning was still, the cool of the night dissipating rapidly under the pressure of the rising sun. Hal stopped long enough to light a cigar, tucked it into the corner of his mouth, and looked across at the end of the long sandbar that stretched back to Cape Pogue Light and East Beach as the sun levered its light down to the earth. Fire, water, land, and air. Only on the coast could you get in touch with the basic elements.

He pulled in enough line to cause the fly to surface and then rolled a long cast out into the deep blue of the fast running current. When he saw the swirl he set the hook and whooped like a wild man as the blue took off at full speed.

A blue, unlike a striper, fights with everything it's got. For fifteen or twenty minutes the pressure never lets up, unless the fish decides to jump, and even then the strain is enormous, bending a stout fly rod right to the butt. They slash, they dive, they run, they leap, and if you can hold them, at the end, they just seem to collapse, and you can lead them to shore.

Hal's fish was a fat five-pounder, and even as he was fighting the fish Rob hooked up and then Carl. For the next hour and a half they were hooked up nearly constantly, taking fish after fish, whooping and hollering each time a fish hammered their flies. They all carried a large pair of pliers to get the hooks out because blues come equipped with very efficient teeth, and more than one fisherman has gotten his fingers slashed while trying to remove a hook.

Then it was over. The fish had moved on out into Nantucket Sound. They knew the fish were gone, but for another hour or so they worked their flies until the tide had run over halfway out and the fishing had truly come to an end.

Carl wound in his line, clipped off the fly, and began stowing his gear. "Now comes the hard part," he said. "It looks like three trips apiece." He turned to Hal and smiled. "The good news is that the old guys only have to carry their gear," he said. "Leave the heavy lugging to the young bucks."

Hal looked up at the steeply rising bank. "Won't hurt my feelings any."

As he carried the last two fish up the long stairs, Rob stopped to catch his breath, looking absently in toward the pond. A piece of hull lying in the grass caught his eye and he decided to go get it after he dropped the fish at the truck where Carl was carefully storing them in ice.

"I gotta check something," Rob said. "I'll be right back."

Carl stopped and looked at him as he weighed his responsibilities. "Where you going?"

"Just down the gut a short way."

Carl walked to the edge of the bank and looked carefully, scanning every piece of cover he could find. It looked safe enough. There wasn't a soul around, but there were God's own amount of places to hide. "Okay," he said, "but keep your eyes open."

Rob nodded and climbed down the stairs. For anyone with a rifle he was an easy target, but they had seen no one nor even any sign of anyone. Still, they hadn't been watching either. They'd been fishing, concentrating on the water and the blues. He thought they must have made pretty good targets then, and down at the bottom they'd been some distance from the truck. It would have been the ideal time. He decided that meant no one was watching.

He tried to put it out of his mind, but he could not. It was just something he had never come up against before. Who ever thought about being a target, about having someone out there trying to kill you, just waiting to get a clear shot? He swiveled his head first one way and then the other as he walked quickly down to where he had seen the piece of wood. How long could you stay on full alert like this without getting a little gamey?

The piece of flotsam wasn't very large, only three boards wide, and a couple of feet long, but there was no doubt in his mind that it had come from the same boat. He picked it up and carried it back down the cut and then up the hill to the truck where he set it on the open tailgate.

"What's that?" Carl asked.

"More of that blown-up boat?" Hal asked.

"I think so," Rob said. "You can see the blast marks."

Carl looked at the piece of hull. "Came from a Swanson by the way the planks are joined," he said. "An old boat."

"How old?" Rob asked.

"At least fifty years." He pointed to the edge of the planks. "When this boat was built they were using old growth cedar and the wood was so dense they could use thinner planks. Now the stock is a quarter of an inch thicker." He ran his fingers over the wood. "It's been painted recently, no more than a month ago, but it wasn't in very good shape." He flipped it over, putting the painted side down, and took out his pocket knife. He opened the knife and stabbed it easily into the wood. "Dry rot."

"What does that mean?" Hal asked.

"I don't know," Carl said. He turned to Rob. "Didn't you say the Coast Guard has the rest of the pieces?"

"Not all of them. Not even half," Rob said.

"We'll drop this off on the way home," Carl said.

"Not until we eat." Rob stepped around to the side of the

truck and pulled the cooler and the sack with the Thermoses to the tailgate. "Mom packs a terrific lunch," he said.

Carl laughed. "He eats like a gull. Got to have something every hour or his stomach begins to digest itself."

"You mean you guys aren't hungry?" Rob said.

"Didn't say that." Carl looked into the open sandwich cooler, and turned to Hal. "Help yourself," he said.

For a while, through several bites of sandwich and swallows of coffee, they said nothing. Finally, Hal finished chewing a bite of his thick ham sandwich, and looked around at Rob. "How did you know the fish were here? I mean, I know what you said, but is it really that simple?"

Rob grinned and then shrugged. "I think like a bluefish when I'm after blues, like a striper when I'm after stripers."

Hal laughed. "Does that mean you're keeping it secret?"

"It means he doesn't know," Carl said. "But he's also spent a lot of time listening to both of our grandfathers, and nobody on this island knows fish better than those two."

"They're both in their seventies, but we still fish, though mostly from the boat ... when we have one," Rob said.

"I meant to tell you," Carl said. "Dad got the insurance check and I got a line on another boat. Have to go up to Jonesboro to get it, but it's supposed to be in mint condition. "I'm going next week. If it's what they say it is, I'll have it hauled to Woods Hole. That way I won't have to have someone drive the truck back."

"All right!" Rob banged his fist down onto the tailgate of

the truck. "I was afraid we were gonna be without a boat, and when the blues move offshore that would have sucked big time."

"I wanted to ask, Rob," Hal said, "after what happened last Saturday, I mean, ah...."

"I'm okay," Rob said.

Hal nodded, but said nothing.

Under different circumstances, Rob would have left it there. But this was, after all, Mallory's father. "I felt pretty awful for a couple of days," he said, "but now it's almost like it never happened. I can still hear the sound of the ball as it hit the guy's head." He shook his head slowly from side to side, his blond hair flopping gently. "I don't ever want to hear that sound again."

"I guess you won't need counseling then," Hal said.

"Dad told me about Viet Nam, and how sometimes you just do what you have to because there's no other choice."

"Besides, you did the world a favor," Carl said. "The guy had a record as long as surf rod. There were two warrants out on him, both for murder, one here and one in Florida. He was one bad dude."

Hal nodded, and Rob could see that he wasn't convinced that there might not have been another way. At first it pissed him off, but as he thought about it, he understood that what was really at issue here was Mallory, and whether he wanted his daughter seeing a guy who had killed a man and did not appear to have any great regrets. And the truth was, he didn't regret it at all. He'd moved past it. What had happened was over, and he knew that if he found himself in a bind like that again, he would react just as quickly. It was the difference between being dead or alive. But he wondered whether you could ever know that unless you had been there. The other thing Hal didn't know was what had happened with Mallory, or if he did, he let it go past without comment. Fine by me, Rob thought. Mallory's got nothing to do with any of this. And with that notion another brick went into the emotional wall he was building around himself.

"He was trying to kill me," Rob said.

Hal reacted quickly. "I'm sorry, Rob, I wasn't there. I have no right to question what you did."

"I just wanted to keep from being shot and he had me pinned down. I wasn't trying to kill him."

Hal grinned. "Hey, you don't have to explain ... no ... I'm sorry, that's what I was asking for, wasn't it?" He shook his head. "Fathers of daughters," he said.

"I can see why you would need to know more," Rob said. "Especially after the press got hold of it and turned me into some kind of hero."

"You don't think you were?" Hal asked.

"I was just trying to keep from getting killed."

"The hero part came later," Carl said, "at the fire when he grabbed me, and threw us both into the harbor just before the boat exploded. If he hadn't done that, I wouldn't be here."

"I hadn't heard about that," Hal said.

"I asked the guys from the fire station not to say anything,"

Rob said.

"Not ready to be a hero?"

Rob shrugged. "I just want to fish and throw baseballs. For now that's enough." It wasn't, because he hadn't mentioned Mallory, but he thought, somehow, Hal either understood or he wasn't ready to say anything.

"I'm sorry, Rob, I should have known better than to ask. Nobody can judge a thing like that unless they were there."

Rob smiled. "It's okay," he said. "But I couldn't have done it any differently. I think it's the way I was brought up. You get into trouble, you get yourself out. If you're gonna spend any time on the water, you have to understand that."

Hal nodded. It was true. He knew it was true because he had been raised the same way on a farm in upstate New York. You had to be self sufficient. You had to be able to deal with whatever happened. But for most of his life he had lived in a different sort of society, a society where you depended on the government to take care of such things, even though they never could. It was all an illusion. An old quote from the Bible popped into his head. How many times had he heard his father say it? Thousands? "God helps those who help themselves."

He looked over at Rob. "I don't think anyone could have handled that situation any better than you did, Rob."

He grinned at Hal. "Now, I just have to convince the rest of the world. You can't believe the reactions of my teachers. They've turned me into some kind of pariah."

"It's a lot to understand," Hal said.

"They're mostly just horror-struck," Rob said.

"Everything from books and nothing from life," Carl said.

"Not everyone can live on the edge," Hal said.

"But that's where we are," Rob said. "Like all the other animals, we wait at the edges before stepping into the open to feed."

Hal looked around at him, thinking about the deer on the farm and how they always waited in the brushy rim at the edges of the fields. "They'll get over it in time," he said.

"Time. Now, that's something I've got a lot of," Rob said.

And that, Hal thought, was something only a kid who loved to fish could understand.

14
Digging Deeper

Chief Platt looked at the piece of hull that Rob and Carl had brought him, carried it out back, and fit it to the other pieces. Rob was surprised by how much more they had found.

"It just keeps turning up," Chief Platt said. "A piece here, a piece there. We even found the piece with the manufacturer's number. It's a Swanson, just as you thought, Rob, and it was built five years ago."

Carl shook his head. "More like fifty years ago." He explained his theory about the thickness of the wood, and showed Chief Platt how badly the wood had dry-rotted.

"Well, that raises a mystery all right," the chief said. "I thought this was a gang rub-out. But maybe that's only what they wanted me to think. I mean, I located a Swanson stolen from a marina in Connecticut, and the manufacturer's ID number matched. The insurance company sent a guy out to look at it. He was here yesterday morning. Everything checked out."

"But what they really did," Rob said. "Was find an old Swanson rotting away in a boat yard somewhere, carve the new number into it, paint it up, tow it out, and blow it up."

"Why go to so much trouble?" Carl asked. "If you wanted to collect on the insurance, just blow it up."

Chief Platt pushed his cap back on his head. "But suppose what you really wanted to do was steal the boat, change the numbers, blow up the old one, and sell the newer one? Or maybe it wasn't stolen. Maybe the owner is in on it, and he collects on the insurance, and gets a cut of the sale of the boat."

"What are the state cops saying?" Carl asked.

"Officially, the guy in the boat died in either a Mafia rub-out or some kind of drug deal that went bad."

"What does that mean?" Rob asked.

"It means they're gonna forget about it. My guess is that they'll go the same route on the guy you popped the other night. They'll call it a case of self-defense brought on by road rage. If that happens, it probably means they've been told from above to forget about it." He looked at each of them carefully, his eyes narrowed. "Which means you guys should forget about it too."

Carl scratched his head. "Why do you think they blew up our boat?"

"A warning I think, but maybe more than that. The blast could easily have been triggered by a radio signal, even a cell phone. One thing's sure. It's the same guys, by the way the bottom was blown out."

Rob's eyes opened very wide. "That's how I knew!" he said. "I saw the Primacord on the hull, but I didn't remember that until just now! Talk about dumb. I knew I'd seen something, but I couldn't remember what it was."

"Can you tell me what it looked like?" Chief Platt asked.

"All I can remember is seeing a thin dark line along the waterline, then I grabbed Carl and the boat went up."

"They must have used a diver to place the charges," Chief Platt said. "Very professional stuff. We didn't find much, just the bottom of the hull and the engine. We're planning to pull that up next week." He grinned. "You're lucky you won't have to pay for the salvage. It's in the channel so we have to take care of it."

"All I want is the engine," Carl said. "Just clean it up, it'll be good as new."

"Even after sitting on the bottom?" Rob asked.

"Diesel," Carl said. "Everything's covered with oil."

"We'll set everything in the yard out front," Chief Platt said.

"Give me a call and I'll get it out of your way. Denny'll let me use his shop to work on it."

"And don't forget what I said. You guys are out of this."

They both nodded.

On the drive home, neither of them said much until they were about a mile from the house.

"You know what I think," Rob said, "I think there's two deals going down at once."

"Forget about it," Carl said. "You got plenty to do."

"Yeah, but ...."

"No buts, here, Rob. You heard what the chief said. These guys will kill anybody who gets in their way, and you, of all people, ought to know that by now."

"It's hard not to think about it. I mean it's like a mystery novel, and I want to find out what happens in the end."

"But it's not a novel, Rob. It's real. It's absolutely real. In a deal like this you pull your head down and wait till it goes by. You stick your head up, they won't miss the next time."

Rob looked down at the floor of the truck, his lower lip projecting slightly. "It just isn't right."

"You know that, I know that, but it doesn't matter! Have you got that, Rob? I mean have you really got that?"

"Yeah." He sighed.

"Get it out of your mind and play ball. Jesus, Rob, for the first time in your life, you've really got things going your way! Don't screw that up!"

"Okay, I got the message!"

"I hope so," Carl said. "After all, you've got the first chance of anybody in either family to be somebody famous, and I'd like to see you play that out."

"What? Famous for what?"

"Baseball, goon ball. What do you think?"

"Do you really think I'm that good?"

"Put it together, Rob. Why did Hal have a Mets pitching coach come all the way up here? I mean, he's a nice guy and all, but that goes beyond the limits of nice guy."

"You're making me nervous."

"Good. This is the time to get nervous so you get it out of your system before you make the next step up."

"What step?"

"Maybe you could play in the Cape Cod League this summer, go to college in the fall, and play there in the spring. "

"Whoa. That is a long way off, you know?"

"Not so far away as you think. You saw the scouts in the stands the other day, right?"

"I did." He laughed. "Scared me too."

"Like I said before, that's good. Every time you have to overcome something like that, it's easier the next time."

"I don't know, Carl. I was pretty scared. Did you notice I didn't recover until they'd left?"

"Yeah, I noticed. But I also noticed you didn't wet your pants, so you couldn't have been too scared."

Rob laughed. "I was until I remembered the stone."

"Look, Rob, you gotta be clear on this. Whatever's going on with these boats, forget it. It'll get solved or it won't, but all you can do is lose. I mean how much closer can you come than you did last week?"

Rob shook his head. "That was pretty close," he said. Carl was right. He had to put it away. There was no choice. He thought about Mallory and the way she smiled and he put that out of his mind, and then he pushed the rest of it as far away as he could. That lasted until they reached the house. There were two black cars in the yard. One of them flew an admiral's flag up front, and both of them carried government license plates.

"This ought to be interesting," Carl said.

"What do you think they want?" Rob asked.

"You been fishing out around Nomans again?"

"Naw. I told you. We went over to Quicks Hole, that's all."

They were sitting in the living room with his parents and they stood as he and Carl entered, and introduced themselves.

Admiral Clayton Stone, a man of medium height with nearly white hair and clear blue eyes, shook hands with Rob and Carl, and you couldn't help but be impressed by all the gold on the sleeves of his uniform and the perfect rows of ribbons.

Next was a man, also in uniform, Commander John Brown from Naval intelligence. The last two, Jim Hurst and Brant Colello wore dark suits, but did not say which agency they were from.

George carried two straight backed chairs in from the dining room and Rob and Carl sat down facing the four men.

"The reason for our visit," Admiral Stone said, "is, as I told your folks, to find out exactly what you saw on Nomans Land. We need to know that because the project we have going out there is top secret, and we have to know if that secrecy has been compromised."

Rob looked directly into the man's eyes. "I haven't fished out there in two years," he said. "I've thought about it, but Dad told me to stay away from there."

"We had a reliable report," Jim Hurst said, "that your boat was seen going at slow speed around the island."

Rob shrugged. "Must not have been too reliable."

"What were you doing out there?" Hurst asked.

"When?" Rob asked. He reached up and scratched the back of his neck. Something was out of whack here, but he couldn't put his finger on it.

"So you were out there," Hurst said, looking very pleased with himself.

"In August, two years ago," Rob said, "but not since."

"Those waters are off limits. Do you usually violate the laws that way?" Colello asked.

"Once the Navy stopped dropping bombs out there," Rob said, "people started fishing the waters around the island. Some years that's the first place the blues show up. A few weeks ago I went over to Quicks Hole and on the way back I took the boat out around Gay Head and glassed the beaches for birds. I also glassed Nomans, but it was too far away to see anything. Then I started up the boat and went home."

"So you admit you went inside the limits," Hurst said.

Rob shook his head. What were they up to? What were they really after? "No. I told you where I went."

"So you willingly violated the limits posted on the charts?"

Rob reached into his pocket and wrapped his fingers about the smooth white piece of quartz. "You heard what I said."

"I think, gentlemen," George said, "you heard my son say he was there two years ago. Is that the date of your report?"

No one spoke.

"I asked you a question," George said.

Admiral Stone smiled and stood up. "We apologize for the nature of our questions," he said. "It seems we're barking up the wrong tree, after all."

They all stood and Rob looked at the rows of ribbons, wondering what they were for, and then he looked hard into Admiral Stone's eyes. They showed no emotion. With not another word spoken, the men left the house and drove away.

"What the hell was that all about?" Carl asked.

"A fishing expedition," George said. He looked around at Carl. "Did you catch it?" he asked.

"It took me awhile."

"What?" Rob asked.

"His medals," George said. "He had his Silver Star ahead of his Navy Cross, and he was wearing a Distinguished Flying Cross, but he had no wings above his ribbons."

"Who are they?" Rob asked.

"I don't know, but somebody thinks you saw something," his father said. "Are you sure you haven't been out to Nomans?"

"Not since I got to know Chief Platt," Rob said.

"There are no bad spots in the log, Dad. Engine hours and trips match up ... or at least they did. I checked it two days before the fire."

Rob stuffed his hands into his pockets. "You mind if I go over to Tom's for awhile?"

"No, go ahead. I think it's safe enough now. They got what they came for."

The new windshield in the Jeep made it feel as if he were driving a new car. Everything was clearer and sharper, and he wondered how he had even been able to see through it before with all the millions of tiny nicks in the glass from windblown sand. It was the fate of any vehicle that spent much time on the beach, but you never noticed it until suddenly it was hard to see though, and the oncoming headlights at night made big coronas in the glass. And now it was clear. He only wished this business about the boats was clear, not to mention his relationship with Mallory, and the SATs, and college, and just what was he going to do come June when high school suddenly spit him out into the world?

Maybe that's why you went to college. It gave you another four years before you had to make the decision. But the way he saw it, the best way to put off making a decision was to grab a rod and go fishing. Nobody could say you weren't doing something productive, no matter how much fun you had.

He stopped in Tom's driveway and climbed out. It didn't matter that he'd already spent a big chunk of the morning fishing, he was always ready for more.

Tom came out carrying a cup of coffee. "What's up?"

"You wanna go fishing?"

"Sure. Where?"

"Philbin."

"Cool. You had lunch?"

"I was gonna pick up something."

"Naw. Mom just bought all kinds of cold cuts."

They tromped into the house and into the kitchen. "We nailed them this morning at Pogue," Rob said.

"And you didn't take me?"

"I figured you didn't get home till late. We got up at three, and besides, it was all fly fishing."

"I'm glad you didn't call." Tom set the packages of cold cuts on the table, and then a loaf of bread and a jar of mayo. "You need anything else?"

"Yeah, you got any pickles?"

They began making sandwiches. "Remember when we got chased by that Cigarette boat?"

"You're serious, right? You think I'd forget?"

"What I mean is, can you think of anything we did that got their attention?"

"No." Tom lathered the bread with mayo and then slabbed four pieces of bologna onto the bread. "All we did was come across, make a swing out past Gay Head, and then they started to chase us."

"We came all the way around the Head," Rob said, "and then we hove to and drifted for a bit, while I glassed the water for birds. Is that right?"

Tom shrugged. "So what?"

"I don't know." He reached for the ham and then added a layer of Swiss cheese. "I just can't figure out why they would have chased us."

"Maybe because of the boat we saw blow up."

"But why? I mean, what could we have seen even if we'd been right there? And we were several miles away." He opened the jar and pulled out a fat dill pickle. "I came well past the Head so I could see all the way down to Squibnocket." He bit into the pickle. "But something we did got that Cigarette boat on our wake."

"You got any bait?" Tom asked.

"We'll stop in Menemsha."

"Too bright to fish the surface," Tom said.

"At least the tide's right," Rob said.

"We've caught a lot of big fish off the bottom there when the tide's running right."

"And we know the bass and blues are around."

"Might even be a tautog or two," Rob said.

"You can't ever be sure what you'll catch in those waters when the tide is right."

15

Eureka! ... Maybe ...

They stopped in the parking lot at Philbin Beach, and they hadn't even unloaded the gear before an Aquinnah cop slipped into the parking lot and drove to where they had piled the gear.

Johnny Belgeddes climbed out and walked toward them, swaggering as if he were a big-time cop in a big-time place.

"So, what's going on here?" he asked, standing with his thumbs hooked in his belt.

"Fishing," Rob said.

"And what makes you think you can park here?"

"John," Tom said. "You know Rob's got a sticker?"

"Watch your mouth, Kincaid."

Rob shook his head, opened the flap on his shirt and pulled out his cell phone. "Look, Belgeddes, you ragged me all last summer and this year I'm not putting up with it, is that clear? I've got a sticker that says I can be here, and unless you want to talk to Mr. Stickwalker, just leave us alone."

"It's not you, it's Kincaid. He doesn't have a pass."

"Nice try, John," Tom said. "What? You been hanging out with The Ultimate Onager in your free time?"

"Who?"

"Onager," Rob said.

"Our departments cooperate, you know, and he put out a warning about you, English. He says you're dangerous and need to be watched." He looked down at his clipboard. "It says you should be stopped and checked for drugs at every opportunity."

Tom laughed. "Sounds like a lawsuit in the making, Robbo. Can I have a copy of that release?"

"Classified police business."

Rob closed up the Jeep and began picking up the gear.

"Where do you think you're going?" Belgeddes said.

"Fishing," Rob said. "I thought we'd been over that."

"No permit, no fishing."

Rob set down the gear, pulled out the phone, and punched in a number, pushed the send button, and held the phone to his ear. "Hello, Mr. Stickwalker, this is Rob English. Tom Kincaid and I are out here at Philbin getting ready to go fishing and Officer Belgeddes is telling me Tom has to have a permit. Yes, sir. Got it the first week of January. Yes, sir, he's right here." He handed the phone to Belgeddes. "Boss wants to talk to you."

Belgeddes took the phone and they could hear Stickwalker shouting at him. All he said at the end was "yes, sir," and then he handed the phone back to Rob.

"Let me tell you something, wise-ass," he pointed his index finger at Rob. "I don't take kindly to people who get me in trouble with my boss."

"And I don't take kindly to cops who push their weight around because they're cops," Rob said. "Just cause you're one eighth Native American you think you own everything out here now, but as far as I'm, concerned you're just another beach skunk. Hell, you weren't even born here."

"You're really beginning to piss me off, English."

"Yeah, I know that," Rob said. "I was kind of afraid you weren't getting the point."

"Hey! Time out!" Tom said. "What is this all about, John?"

"I told you we got a warning."

"From Onager, the dumbest slug on the whole Island. Why would you listen to him? I don't get it."

"He's a cop," Belgeddes said.

"Oh, we knew that all right," Tom said, "just based on the number of doughnuts he eats."

"Onager says you found that body."

"So?"

"You know who the guy was?"

"Yeah. Josh Warner."

"Now, how do you know that when the State Police haven't issued their report yet?"

"I recognized his clothes. He's the only guy on the Island who dresses like that."

It stopped him. The pure truth of it stopped him. "He was my cousin."

"And Onager told you I must have had something to do with his dying."

"Yeah."

"John," Rob said, "I think you oughta go have a talk with Chief Platt. He says that what they did to Josh is a mark left by some big time drug cartel. He saw it a lot down in Florida."

"It was awful what they did to him."

Rob nodded. "And maybe you ought to talk to Paul Bianca about Onager, 'cause I gotta tell you, John, this is dumb."

"You heard about what happened, didn't you?" Tom asked. "About the baseball."

"Yeah. I was there, John. They were trying to kill us!"

"Why would anybody do that? It doesn't make any sense," Belgeddes said. He shook his head and looked down at his clipboard. "Maybe you guys could do me a favor. I got a call from Billy Brightmoon. There's a report about some guys diving for lobsters out where he sets his pots. He asked me to keep a lookout for a dive boat. You guys are gonna be out here fishing, and maybe you could give me a call if you saw anything."

Rob nodded. It was over and there was no sense in doing anything but mending fences. "Sure, we could do that," he said. "Billy's pots are just this side of the Head, aren't they?"

"Yeah, but you can only see them from the beach."

"We'll keep a lookout," Tom said.

"I'm sorry about giving you such a hard time," John said. "I don't know Onager all that well. I just thought I was getting a police report, you know? But what I don't get is how come you know Stickwalker so good?"

"Family's been here a long, long time," Rob said. "And

Dad's pretty tight with the Tribe too. And then there's the fact that my great-great grandmother was a Narragansett."

"And Stickwalker knows that."

"Sure."

He grinned again and stuck out his hand. "Hey, no hard feelings, okay?"

They both shook hands with him. "It's forgotten," Rob said.

"Me too," Tom said.

They picked up their stuff and walked down to the beach, turning toward the Head, and stopping near a large cluster of boulders. They could hardly have been more alone. All the houses back by the road were closed for the winter, and there wasn't a soul on the beach in either direction.

The tide was coming in and the wind, setting from the north, blew out over their heads, leaving them in the glow of the afternoon sun. They sat learning against the warmth of a big rock, waiting for the tide, and watching the gulls slide along the edge of the water, riding the wind, their wings still.

"Do you believe that guy?" Tom said. "How could anyone take Onager seriously?"

"It's just the Aquinnah attitude," Rob said. "They don't want anyone out here."

"But they want their money."

"It doesn't make any sense to me. They could put a parking strip the whole way down Lobsterville and sell season permits and make a bundle. Every fisherman on the Island would have to have one. Look at the number of people who buy vehicle permits for the beaches. They could even have two sections, one for Islanders and one for tourists."

"I'd sure like to be a Pequot or a Mohegan," Tom said. "Those guys are rolling in money."

Rob smiled. "Hey, if the Narragansetts get it going, we could be chopping in tall cotton. Dad is a full eighth and gramps is a quarter."

"Now there's another thing I never knew about you. How come I never knew that?"

"My grandfather told me two weeks ago. He's convinced I'm the next Jim Thorpe, or I would be if I had more native blood in me and I came from the right tribe."

"Does being an Indian explain the trick with the stones?"

Rob shrugged. "Got me." He looked out at the water. "And by the way," he said, "that's Native American...."

Tom took the bait. "What is this crap? I ..." Then he saw the grin. "Okay, you got me, Robster! I never saw it coming!"

"You ready to catch a fish? Tide's about three quarters."

They rigged their rods quickly, Tom deciding to fish the bottom with a chunk of frozen bunker, while Rob pulled on his new waders and fastened the stripping basket around his waist.

Tom walked down to the water's edge and whipped his long surf rod, sending the chunk of bait and the weight beneath it a long way out. He left the bail off, walked back to the dry sand and the rock, and sat down as he fixed the bail and set the drag on the reel. "Now this is my kind of fishing," he said. "Nothing to do but sit and look at the water and wait for some monster to sniff out my bait."

Rob laughed. "Just don't fall asleep."

"Never happen," Tom said.

Rob walked a little farther up the beach and waded out into the cold water. The beach fell off slowly here, and he was a hundred feet from shore by the time he began to cast. He'd made only one retrieve when he heard the boat, the sound of the engine carried in on the wind. It was a long way off, but he reeled in, and walked back to where Tom sat, sleeping in the sun.

He poked him awake as he opened his big pack and pulled out a sixty-power scope and tripod.

"What's up," Tom asked.

"There's a boat."

"You think it's them?"

"It's coming this way and it's too big to be Billy's." He set the scope up on the shaded side of the rock where no light would reflect from the glass, huddled down behind it, and waited.

The sound grew steadily louder and then they could see the boat, another Cigarette boat, but only about thirty feet long, moving very slowly as a guy in the bow watched for rocks. They stopped about three hundred yards offshore, dropped the anchor, and lowered a diving platform over the side.

"It's them," Tom said.

Rob hunkered down and looked through the scope. "Two men in dry suits." They strapped on tanks, slipped over the side, and disappeared.

"How deep is it out there?" Tom asked.

"I don't know for sure. Forty feet, maybe."

"Would they be going after lobsters in that much water?"

"I don't think so. But I know one thing." He sat up and looked around at Tom. "That boat is anchored pretty close to where we hove to when I was glassing for birds." And then, out of thin air, out of nothing, he understood. "There's a boat down there. They're diving the boat that blew up. The currents are just right to carry the debris around the Head, especially with the wind we had then. It was running south, southeast."

"Hey! One of them just surfaced! And there's the other one!"

Rob looked through the scope. Each man was towing something in a net bag and as he watched they reached the boat, climbed up onto the platform, loaded the nets into the boat, and climbed aboard."

"What did they bring up? Could you see it?"

"No. All I could see were the nets. It didn't look too heavy, though." He pulled the scope back behind the rock. "Don't move. They're scanning the shore with glasses. Just keep down."

And then the drag on Tom's reel began to buzz as a fish took the bait.

"Damn," Tom said. He watched the line disappearing from the reel. "I gotta get it. When it reaches the end the whole rig will go sailing over the beach and they'll see it for sure!"

"Be careful."

Tom lay on his belly in the sand, reached around the rock, grabbed the pole by the butt, and slowly pulled it toward him. He rolled onto his side, keeping the rod low and horizontal to the ground. "Jeez, it's a big fish!" He tightened the drag knowing he was close to the breaking point. Seconds later he knew he either had to tighten the drag again and let the fish break off, or loosen it a half turn and try to fight it. The sound of the boat engine saved him . He loosened the drag and gave the fish line. Behind him he could hear Rob talking to Chief Platt.

"If they stay on course, they're headed into Woods Hole."

"Rob! Hey, Rob!"

"Two men, thirty-foot boat, maroon and white, and making probably fifty knots. Yeah, okay."

"Jeez, Tom, what are you doing?" Rob asked as he watched Tom fighting the fish while lying on his side. "A fish that big doesn't need any help."

Tom rolled onto his feet, and now with the rod up and able to use his weight, he began gaining line. "I don't think it's all that big."

"Pretty big," Rob said. "I'm gonna guess twenty pounds."

"I can live with that! First big fish this early in the season? Man, this is gonna be a year!"

Not until Tom had played the big fish out and they hauled it up onto the beach and killed it, did they settle down. "That's the biggest blue I ever caught!" Tom said. "I'll bet that's as big as the one that won the Derby last year." He stopped and looked up at Rob. "What happened to the boat?"

"Chief Platt has him on radar from one of the ferries and they're coming out with the big cutter from Woods Hole, but there's a lot of places he can go. The trick is to let him land and

185

nail him. If they try to get him at sea, he'll dump the cargo, and they'll never find it." He stripped his waders down. "The only thing that bothers me is that they took off so fast. I'm sure they didn't see us, but I wasn't watching. I think we better get back to the Jeep and lay low for awhile until we see what happens."

"Is Poole's buying fish?"

"Yeah, but I don't think we want to be seen around there just now. I think you'll have to eat this one."

Tom shrugged. "Won't hurt my feelings," he said.

16

Suspicion

Tom and Rob burst through the door of the Coast Guard station and stopped at the front desk.

"Did you get them?" Rob asked.

Chief Platt shook his head. "Nope."

"I thought you said you had them on radar."

"We tracked it all the way across and stopped them in the marina, but they were clean. Nothing."

"Go figure," Tom said in disbelief.

"What did they do, throw the stuff overboard?"

Chief Platt shrugged and sat back in his chair.

"You're sure it was the right boat," Rob said.

The chief sat forward in his chair and looked down at the sheet of paper on his desk. "Thirty foot, white and maroon Cigarette boat. Two men, both wearing dry suits. They said they'd been diving for lobsters, for which they had a license."

"And no lobsters."

"Right, not a one." He brushed his right hand over his thick dark crew cut. "I was pretty sure you had come up with something. Now I don't know what to say."

"They searched the boat?"

"Even had a drug-sniffing dog with them."

"What do you figure," Tom asked, "a buoy somewhere with a radio beacon?"

"Could be that. But there was no reason to take the risk unless they knew they'd been seen."

"I'm sure they didn't see us," Rob said, "but guys like that, professionals, they're probably darn good at what they do."

"Their freedom and their profit depend on it," Chief Platt said. "Every time we think we got them figured out, they come up with a new scheme. They've got God's own amount of money. They can afford to hire smart guys."

"I never thought of that," Rob said. "I thought it was like the movies where the crooks are kinda dumb."

"Sure make my job a whole lot easier," the chief said.

"At least we found out one thing," Rob said. "We know where that other boat blew up." He looked down at the chart on the counter under glass. "Right here," he said, putting his finger on the glass, "give or take a couple of hundred feet."

Chief Platt got up and walked over to the counter. "Interesting idea. They sink a boat with a load of dope on it, and then they bring it up whenever they need it. They could have boats on the bottom all up and down the coast with the dope in sealed packages, just lying there on the bottom in weighted bags."

"That's why they chased us. This is very close to where Tom and I hove to that day to glass the shore for birds. They must've thought we knew something, but it was pure coincidence."

Chief Platt looked at the depth number on the chart. "Forty-two feet. That's a lot of water."

"On the ebb there aren't any currents running."

"It's worth checking," Chief Platt said. "I'll take the cutter over and see if we can pick up something on the sonar."

"I think you'll have to dive it," Rob said. "They blew the bottom out of the boat, everything above that floated away."

The chief nodded. "So the sonar probably won't separate it from the bottom."

"Right."

"They'd need to get right to the spot to make a pick up, so maybe they dropped a beacon. We'll scan for that too."

"What about the other boat?" Tom asked. "Did they dive that one yet?"

"I don't think so."

"They won't find anything," Rob said. "They cleaned that off as soon as no one was around."

"I'm sure you're right, but we need to send divers down anyway, just to see if they blew the boat the same way."

Rob grinned at Tom. "I guess we're clear to sell your fish."

"Let's go, then. I need the cash."

They had just come out of Larson's when Rob suddenly stopped. "Wait a minute! I know what they did. Listen, they probably figured they could be tracked by radar anywhere in Vineyard Sound as soon as they stood out from shore, right? And it wouldn't make much sense to throw the stuff overboard a second time because of the risk. So they must've had a second boat waiting. But that boat didn't cross. The stuff is still here."

"It's a pretty big island, Rob."

"Yeah, but there aren't many places to put in a boat that size without someone noticing it. And they could have put in close to shore and screened themselves from the radar just long enough to transfer the stuff."

"So we go looking for another boat in Vineyard Haven, Oak Bluffs, and Edgartown."

"Right." They climbed into the Jeep.

"What kind of a boat would we be looking for?"

"A sport fisherman, because they could take ice chests off without anyone noticing." He put the Jeep in gear and hammered down the accelerator. "I think we need to take a guess between the three." He looked at his watch. "They've got a forty-five minute head start, but they'd have no reason to run at full speed, and it would only attract attention."

"Oak Bluffs," Tom said.

"Okay, but why?"

"Because there are more boats in the water there."

"And that would give them better cover."

"Right."

"Oak Bluffs, here we come. All we gotta do is avoid The Ultimate Onager."

"Not to mention Donny and then the West Tisbury guys and then the Tisbury guys."

They got lucky, almost no traffic and not a cop in sight. Even so Rob would not drive over fifty, if only because you could never tell when someone would come popping out of a side road. They got lucky again in Vineyard Haven, getting there between ferries and the spate of traffic they always produced.

In Oak Bluffs they swung around to the water and parked out where the people ferry ties up. They scanned the harbor for any boat that was open, but every boat had been secured. All they could do was wait.

"I didn't see Onager anywhere," Tom said. "He's usually around on Saturday afternoons."

"Probably cuddled up with a sack of chocolate creams."

Tom laughed. "Did you ever watch him eat one? He, like, makes love to it. Man, is it gross. I watched him once and I swore I'd never eat a chocolate cream again."

"He must spend half his pay on doughnuts."

"Hey," Tom said, "did you ever hear from that girl again?"

"Yup."

"Whoa, that doesn't sound good."

"Turns out she's got a boyfriend."

"Sure can't be serious from the way she kissed you."

Rob shrugged. "I don't what to make of stuff like that."

"Nobody does. You just have to wait and see where it goes. It's like fishing. You put out the bait and make sure they know it's there, and then you wait. At least that's what my Dad says, but he's kind of cynical."

"Cynical or not, it sounds right. Makes me feel helpless."

"I think that's just what they want."

"I don't get you."

"I mean, they want you to be waiting around until they decide. The way to beat it is write her a letter saying you're going out with someone else."

"I don't know if I could do that."

"Sure you could."

"It isn't very honest."

"Honesty's got nothing to do with this, Robbo. This is war, man! Look, Melissa had me tied in knots and finally Dad sat me down and explained some stuff. Mostly, I never listen to him, but this was man-to-man. It wasn't like a lecture at all. Dad's pretty smart, you know."

"Yeah I know. But then he's a doctor, and doctors are supposed to be smart."

"He even poured me a beer."

"Really?"

"Yeah, really. And here's what he said. He said women never know what they want so you have to help them make up their mind. Usually they want most what they can't have."

"We're all like that, Tom."

"But it's not the same for women. Dad says a man can set goals, and when he reaches those goals he can be content for a long time. But a woman gets there, and then she wants more. He says a lot of divorces happen because of that."

"You're making my head spin here. How come I never read anything like this?"

"I don't know. All I know is what Dad said, and when I thought about how Melissa kept jerking me around, I knew he was right. Then I had to decide whether I liked her enough to make her want me. I mean, I'm a good guy, okay? I wouldn't want to hurt someone just to win. I wanted to be sure that when I won, I was satisfied."

"Are you?"

He laughed. "I don't know. I thought I did, and I was sure I would, but I still don't know."

"Maybe I'll stay with baseball and fishing."

"Did you try talking to her?"

"You mean call her up? I never made a long distance phone call in my life. And anyway, I did something else."

"What?"

"I sent her a copy of *The Taming of the Shrew.*"

"Okay, you're over my head here. What is that?"

"A play by Shakespeare. It's about a really willful girl who refuses to get married."

"Now that's a different approach."

"I was kind of pissed, I guess, and I .... Hey! Look!" He pointed to a sport fisherman rounding into the harbor.

"You think that's them?"

"They came from the right direction, but we'll just have to watch to be sure."

The boat slipped into the harbor, idling along so it threw no wake to rock the other boats, and headed for a slip on the far side. They watched the men unload two ice chests, and then wash down the boat and button up the canvas. Finally they loaded the coolers into the back of a pickup and climbed in.

"Do you know who they are?" Tom asked.

"I never saw them before but it's not like it used to be. There's a lot of new people living here year-round now."

"Yeah. Sucks. Big time."

Rob started the Jeep. "Let's follow them." Neither of them noticed the boat just outside the harbor, idling slowly toward the entrance. They were focused on the dark blue, shiny new Ford F-150. They stayed well behind as the truck crossed the Island and headed toward Edgartown.

It turned off the South Road into one of the new subdivisions, and pulled into a driveway. They stopped well up the street, watching as the men got out, carried the coolers to the front of the house, and opened them. One of the men disappeared inside and came back out with two long filleting knives.

"Fish," Tom said. "The coolers are full of fish!"

They stayed only until the men had emptied the coolers and dumped the ice onto the lawn.

"Barking up the wrong tree," Rob said as he started the Jeep, backed around in a driveway, and headed out to the South Road.

"Or we picked the wrong boat."

"Let's go check the harbor again."

"What a bummer," Tom said. "I thought we had 'em."

"Yeah, so did I," Rob said.

"So tell me more about this play you sent her."

He shrugged. "I thought it would help her make up her mind. I had to do something. I mean, her boyfriend's there, and she sees him all the time, and all I could do is write a letter.

Shows you how dumb I am. I never thought of calling her."

"So now you call her!"

"I don't even know how to get her number."

"Ask her parents."

"Can you do things like that?"

"Whoa. You are really retarded here, Robbo."

"All this stuff is new."

It took them fifteen minutes to cross back to Oak Bluffs, having picked up some weekend traffic, but when they pulled past the marina they saw the boat immediately. It was a sport fisherman, but it was a thirty-nine-foot Bertram, a boat that could move very fast through very rough water.

They drove past and out to the ferry landing and parked. Rob picked up his glasses and checked the boat. "There's a light on in the cabin," he said, "and they've hooked onto the power and water lines on the pier, so they're planning to stay for a while. I can't see much else."

"So what do we do. Wait?"

Rob looked at his watch. "I got an hour before I have to call home or get home in time for dinner. What about you?"

"Two hours. We eat late."

"Let's wait awhile and see if anything happens."

"Too bad you don't have a CD player in this thing."

"Cost too much."

"But you gotta have tunes, man."

"Like who?"

"Like Phish. They are totally awesome."

"Do you really think I should call her?"

"Absolutely. If she's pissed about the book, you'll know right away, and then maybe you can talk it out."

"Talk? What would I say, Tom?"

"Play it by ear. You'll know when the time comes."

But Rob had absolutely no faith in that. "Yeah ... right." He stared absently across the harbor, watching the traffic on the road moving slowly in both directions. Maybe he shouldn't have sent the book. Would she get the wrong idea? He hadn't meant her to think he thought she was a shrew. The point was about making up her mind. But would she see it that way? He began to think that of all the dumb things he had done in his life, this may have been the least intelligent. But each time he thought that, he knew he didn't believe it. She was smart! She was going to a really good college! Wouldn't she be able to figure that out?

"Look," Tom said," there goes The Ultimate Onager." He pointed to an old battered Suburban. "Must be off duty."

"I didn't think he ever went off duty. Every time I look around, he's following me."

"Not today."

They watched him pull up the side road into the marina and stop behind the Bertram.

"What the heck is this!" Rob said as he picked up the glasses.

They watched Onager get out of the Suburban and waddle up to the boat. Then two men came out of the cabin, each of them carrying a cooler. They stepped up onto the pier, carried them to the back of the Suburban, and handed them one at a time to Onager who loaded them into the back.

They all shook hands and laughed and then Onager levered himself back up into the Suburban and drove off.

"Damn!" Rob said.

"What?"

"We can't follow him. He knows my Jeep."

"Do you really think that's dope?"

"I'm sure of it."

"So what do we do?"

"I think we got a problem."

"Why not just go to talk to Bianca?"

"Because he won't believe us."

"Why wouldn't he believe us?"

"He doesn't trust kids, that's why." He started the Jeep and headed for the main road.

"Where are we going?"

"To the source."

"Where?"

"From what I hear, a lot of people visit Wilson's Garage. I've never been there, but that's what I hear. We'll take a short cut, park on a side street, walk back, and see if that's where Onager goes."

"Isn't this getting pretty risky?"

"Not if we're careful."

"I'm getting pretty nervous here, Robbo."

"Me too. But I can't see any other way to do it."

They cut through the tightly set cottages in the old camp-
ground to the far side and parked on a street one short block
from Wilson's. Then they squatted down behind a privet hedge
in front of a cottage closed for the winter and waited.

Minutes later Onager pulled up in front of Wilson's and
stopped. He blew his horn several times, and when nobody
came, he climbed out of the Suburban and walked to the door.
Clearly there was no one home, and he waddled back and
shoved himself up into the Suburban.

"I got an idea," Rob said. "I want to get those coolers."

"Now I know you're nuts."

"You take the Jeep, circle around and go past him at about
forty. Flick him off as you go by. No matter what, he's gonna
chase you, 'cause he'll think it's me. Whip around the corner,
stop and jump out, and open the hood as if you broke down.
While he's busy with you, I'll slip the coolers out of the back of
his Suburban. The next street is a one-way, so he'll have to go a
block up and two blocks over to get back to Wilson's. Just make
sure you stop where there's some cover so if he looks into his
mirrors he won't see anything."

"You really have gone over the edge here, Rob."

"No. It'll work. Just do what I told you."

"You're sure about this."

"All he'll do is give you a ticket. But don't be afraid to give
him some lip to keep him busy. I don't want him looking back."

"Okay, but I don't see what this is gonna get us."

"His fingerprints and the fingerprints of the guys in the boat are on the handles of that chest. We'll take them to Bianca, he'll check the prints and that'll be all the evidence he'll need. That and two witnesses."

"Okay. It's crazy, but I'll do it."

Tom slipped back around the corner using the hedge for protection, got into the Jeep, took a deep breath, and started it. This *was* crazy, he thought, but it was just crazy enough to work.

He came around the corner fast enough to make the tires squeal, roared past Onager, stuck his hand up above the roof, and flicked him off. It was like throwing a plug into a bluefish feeding frenzy. Onager started the Suburban and tore off after the Jeep.

The instant he turned the corner, Rob took off after him on the run. At the corner he slowed to a walk only long enough to watch Onager climb out of the Suburban, and then he took to the street, keeping himself behind the Suburban the whole way.

He opened the door and picked up the first cooler, wrapping his arm around it so he didn't touch the handles, then hid it behind a collection of garbage cans and went back for the second. Onager was about out of his mind, hollering and shouting and waving his arms, and he was totally focused on Tom.

Rob slipped the second cooler out, closed the door, hid the second cooler with the first, and signaled to Tom before slipping out of sight alongside another winter-dormant cottage. He didn't move until he heard the Suburban roar off up the street and turn the corner. When he was sure it was gone, he grabbed the first cooler and carried it to the Jeep, and ran back for the second as Tom closed the hood. With the second cooler in the back, he climbed into the driver's seat.

"Jesus!" Tom shouted. "We did it! We did it! Do you know that? I mean, we did it!"

Yeah," he said. "Did Onager give you a ticket?"

Tom held it up. "I'll have a tough time explaining this."

"Naw. By that time Onager'll be cooling off in the Edgartown pokey." Rob headed out to the Vineyard Haven Road and wasted no time getting to the State Police office.

Shoot The Messenger

17

"Let me get this straight," Trooper Bianca said, looking skeptically at the bags of cocaine now spread on his desk, "you're accusing Officer Onager of being part of a smuggling ring?" His dark brown eyes seemed to bore into them.

"I guess that's what it amounts to," Rob said, "but all we're really saying is what we told you. We saw two guys unload the stuff from a boat, load it into Onager's Suburban, and then he took it to Wilson's Garage. We didn't know what it was until we looked in the coolers, took out a package, and opened the waterproof wrapping."

"And you knew it was cocaine?"

"I never saw cocaine before," Rob said. "But it looked like the stuff you see in the movies, and somehow I didn't think they were all worked up over two coolers of confectionery sugar."

"But you don't know whether it's cocaine."

"Taste it," Tom said. "It's coke."

"How do you know what coke tastes like?"

"There's a lot of kids from cities here in the summer," Tom

said. "Oak Bluffs is full of the stuff. You can get anything you want there in the summer."

"But you're not a doper, right?" Again the skeptical look.

"I tried it once," Tom said. "I didn't like it."

"And you don't use marijuana either, right?"

Tom stared at him. "I didn't inhale," he said.

"Wise guy, too."

"What is this?" Rob asked. "We come in here and hand you a big-time drug bust, and you act like we're the bad guys."

Bianca stood up, walked across the office, turned, and with his thumbs hooked in his gun belt, he stared down at them. "What I've got is your word against that of a police officer."

"And a report from Onager that says Rob here should be stopped and checked for drugs at every opportunity."

Bianca shook his head. "What'd he do, put up wanted posters in the post offices?"

"There's a history," Rob said. "When Onager was in high school he and three of his buddies tried to beat up my brother. Instead he beat up all four of them. Carl was a three-sport athlete and he was real popular, but he came from up-Island. Now Onager's trying to settle an old score."

Bianca nodded, leaning back against the window sill and crossing his arms over his chest.

Tom looked up. "Most of the dope on the Island goes through Wilson's. Everybody but you guys seem to know that."

"So who's to say Officer Onager wasn't gathering evidence? Suppose he set up some kind of a sting."

"Onager?' Rob laughed. "The human doughnut bag?" It was beyond comprehension.

"He's made a lot of arrests," Bianca said.

"Pot shots, right?" Tom asked. "All pot, and never with intent to sell."

"How do you know that?"

"It's in the papers," Rob said.

"How much drugs are there on the Island?"

"Plenty," Tom said. "Ask my Dad. He's a doctor."

"If Onager was collecting evidence, why did he go to Wilson's Garage instead of to the station?" Rob asked.

Bianca nodded. "Good question," he said. "But there could be a logical explanation."

"He probably doesn't inhale either," Rob said.

"You're talking about a police officer here," Bianca said.

"I thought I was talking about a president," Tom said.

"I'll give you this, you guys got cojones all right. Most kids would be shaking in their shoes."

"What's that got to do with Onager?" Rob asked.

"I don't know. You tell me."

"We did," Tom said.

"Maybe you did and maybe you didn't."

"What do you think?" Rob asked. "That we're working some kind of a dodge here? Are you thinking maybe we've got it in for Onager? Is that it? So what? We found two coolers full of coke along the road and decided to use it to hang Onager? "

Bianca walked back to the window. He said nothing for a

long time, and finally Rob broke the silence. "Aren't you going to arrest him?"

"Who? Onager? No. At least not until I have some proof."

"How long is all this going to take?" Rob asked.

"What difference does it make?"

"Once Onager finds out that the coolers are missing," Rob said, "he'll probably run."

"Why would he run?" Bianca asked.

Tom looked at Rob and Rob looked at Tom and they stood up. "I guess we'll go," Rob said.

"Not until I say so," Bianca said.

Rob's temper flared, and he had to squeeze his hands into fists for several seconds to keep himself under control. "Are you arresting us?"

"That's a lot of cocaine...."

"I thought you said it wasn't cocaine," Tom said.

"I said I wasn't certain."

Rob sat down. "Okay, then we'll wait for you to get a lab guy in here to test the stuff, and to take fingerprints from the handles on the coolers. There are at least three sets of prints. Onager's and the two guys on the boat. But every second you wait something's happening. My guess is that without the dope, he's in big trouble. They're not gonna believe he lost it."

Bianca sneered. "It might be a long wait."

Rob stood up. "C'mon, Tom," he said, "let's get out of here."

"You heard what I said. You leave when I tell you."

Rob whipped around and stared at him. "You can't keep

us here without charging us with something. So you'd better arrest us, right now, or we're gone."

Bianca blinked and Rob knew he'd been running a bluff.

"And where are you going?" Bianca asked. "On another private police mission?"

"The Gazette," Rob said. "You may not be interested in this, but I know they are."

And that got Bianca's attention. "Maybe you better listen to me first," he said.

"No," Rob said. "I'm through listening to you. We bring you the biggest bunch of drugs ever taken here, and you accuse of us of being a part of it, and not only doesn't that make any sense, but you call us liars!" In a flash of understanding he knew what was going to happen. "What's more if you don't do something fast, Onager is dead, and there goes your chance to bargain him into ratting out the guys he's in this with."

Bianca ran a hand over his thick short hair. "God, I wish they'd stop putting cop shows on television. Everybody's a cop now. Everybody knows more than the cops." He looked at Rob, studying him carefully. The anger was real, he decided. It was even righteous. "Okay, you say Onager's part of a drug ring. How about you get in the car with me and we'll confront him?" He expected them to back down.

"Suits me," Rob said. "Tom?"

"Sure. But I have to tell my folks where I am."

"Go ahead. Use the phone in the outer office."

Tom left the room and Bianca looked closely at Rob. "You're

sure about this?"

"I'm sure," Rob said. "But we're taking a big risk here. If you believe Onager, he's gonna know who to look for."

"And you're willing to take that risk?"

Tom stepped back into the office. "My father wants to talk to you," he said to Bianca.

They listened from the inner office, but they could hear little of what was said. It lasted several minutes and then Bianca stepped back into the office. "Your father says neither of you can go with me. He says it's too risky, and if what you told me is true, he's right." He crossed the office to a big safe, ran the combination, and opened it up. Without a word he loaded the bags of coke into the safe and swung the heavy steel door closed. Next he took out two stickers that read "Evidence! Do not touch!" and pasted one to each of the coolers.

"Okay. You guys go on home. We'll take it from here." He grinned. "And your father says don't be late for dinner."

They wasted no time getting out to the Jeep.

"Is he gonna do anything?" Tom asked.

"Who knows? The guy's another Onager as far as I know."

"What's the matter with him anyway?"

"Maybe he's part of it," Rob said.

"Oh great! Why didn't we think of that sooner?"

"Because he's a cop ... a state cop. They're supposed to be the good guys."

"So what do we do now?" Tom asked.

"I think we go see Chief Platt."

A half-hour later they walked into the Coast Guard station. There were people running every which way, including some people with a lot of gold on their sleeves.

"Can I help you," an officer asked.

"Is Chief Platt here?" Rob asked.

"He's busy just now."

"We really need to talk to him."

"What about?"

"I'd rather not say but it's very important."

"Look, I'm sorry, but we're really busy just now. If this isn't an emergency, come back later."

Rob lowered his voice. "It is an emergency. Somebody's gonna get killed."

The officer, young, an ensign with but a single gold stripe on his sleeve, looked at them carefully. "Okay. I'll go get him, but this better be good."

Seconds later Chief Platt came out of the back, smiling from ear-to-ear. "We found it," he said, "and it was loaded."

"And we found the other boat," Rob said.

"All right! Where?"

"Can we talk in private?" Rob asked.

"Yeah, sure, but I want my commander to hear this, okay?" Rob nodded.

They sat in a small office with the chief and Commander Carlson, a tall man in his late thirties, with very distant blue eyes. Slowly, they told them what had happened.

Tom took a slip of paper out of his pocket and handed it to

them. "These are the hull numbers and a description of the boat."

"We're on it!" Chief Platt jumped up, took the paper into the outer office, and came rushing back.

"Let me make some calls," Commander Carlson said. "Would you mind waiting outside?"

"No, sir," Rob said.

"Come on," Chief Platt said, "I'll show you what we pulled off the bottom."

It was an impressive pile of bundles, stacked nearly four feet high and in a six by six square.

"That's all dope?" Tom asked.

"Cocaine. This is the biggest haul ever made up here. Only the stuff in Florida comes close." He clapped each one of them on the shoulder. "And you guys are responsible for it. Make you feel pretty good?"

Rob grinned. "Yeah," he said. "I hate this stuff."

"So does my father," Tom said. "He's a doctor and the thing he hates worse than anything is a kid dying of a drug overdose."

"Well, he'll be real proud of you then, Tom. Both of you."

"Do you think Bianca is part of this?"

"No. I think he's a young cop, looking at something very, very big and he wasn't sure how to handle it except to swagger and act tough. I know Paul. He's okay, just young enough to remember what it was like to be a teenager, and knowing how a lot of teenagers act, especially in Boston where he grew up."

They turned as Commander Carlson walked up to them.

"Bianca found Onager. He'd been shot through the head. The good news is that Bianca also arrested the two guys from the boat, and he's got them in the lockup in Edgartown. They had a load of guns on the boat, and one of them was carrying a nine millimeter which may be the gun used to kill Onager.

"Bianca also called in the Oak Bluffs and Edgartown police and they raided Wilson's. The place was full of drugs. It was a crack factory. After Chief Platt called Woods Hole, they sent the chopper on a run out along Nashawena. There were divers working, but nobody on deck. They tracked the boat to New Bedford and the New Bedford cops took it from there. They got the guys on the boat, the delivery guys, and a second crack factory that they've been trying to find for two years." He clapped his hands together. "This is a banner day, and you two men are responsible for it! Genuine heroes!"

"But not famous heroes," Chief Platt said. "Your part in this can never be known."

"Suits me," Rob said. "It nearly got me shot and it did cost us our boat."

"I shouldn't worry about that," Commander Carlson said. "There will be a substantial reward."

"Reward?" Tom grinned. "I can handle that all right!"

18 — One More Game

Tom called for the ball from Chris Hooper at third and walked out to the mound with it tucked tightly into the pocket of his big mitt.

"You ready?"

"Yeah."

He looked carefully at his oldest and best friend and nodded. What he'd seen in his warm up pitches, he saw in his eyes. He was focused. And then he did the unconscionable. He tried to disrupt that focus. "You got your mind on nothing but baseball, right?"

"Nothing."

"All that other stuff is behind us, right?"

"Right."

"What about Mallory?"

"Gone, but not forgotten."

"What about that game last week?"

"Gone, but not forgotten."

Tom grinned. "Okay, then." He handed him the ball, walked back, put his mask on, and squatted as the first batter stepped in. He called for a pitch down the middle, and that's what he got, a steaming fastball, rising up toward the letters, hitting his glove so hard it hurt through both sponges. The roar from the crowd could have been heard in Edgartown.

In the end he was perfect. Not only did no one get on base, but no one even hit a foul ball. Twenty-one batters struck out. He threw sixty-three pitches, and nobody left until the last strike smacked into Tom's mitt, and then the crowd went volcanic. They had just seen what they never expected to see again, and the guy who had done it was one of them. He'd been born here, he grew up here, they'd known him all his life, and most of all they wanted him to remember them, because suddenly it was clear that Rob English's future was off-Island.

But for a while longer, for one short month, he was theirs, he belonged to them the way only home-born heroes belong, and he was a hero in every sense of the word. Who else could throw holes through the air? Who else could have acted so quickly to save his brother? And he was modest and well spoken, and he sounded like where he came from.

He pitched two perfect games back to back, and then he faltered, and for three games he was only human. He won them all, but he gave up hits and runs, like any pitcher does. That was enough to make the scouts nervous about the baseball draft coming up in June. Did you take a chance? Was he a flash in the pan? Would he throw himself out by the time he was twenty? Did he have an attitude problem they couldn't see?

Rob ignored it all. He no longer cared how many people

211

were watching. He focused through it and threw strikes. That he was suddenly not pitching perfect games, he chalked off to one of those strange mysteries that seem to have no answer. He won every game he pitched, and that was all that counted.

The only thing he regretted was having sent Mallory the book. A month had gone by without a letter, and he assumed that whatever he felt for her, she did not feel for him. He said nothing about it to Hal when they went fishing, and Hal offered no information.

If she had just told him at the start, it wouldn't have been so bad. Even if she'd told him later, he could have accepted it. But telling him in a letter was like just brushing him off as if he didn't matter. Some guys might put up with that, he thought, but he wouldn't. No matter how he felt about her, he would not wimp out. He might not, he thought, know much about women, but he knew that however a relationship started, that was the way it would continue. Maybe when summer came and she was here and her boyfriend wasn't, maybe then it would change.

He wondered if that was what had happened to his pitching. Maybe he was just spending too much time thinking about it. And maybe that's why he was tired all the time? Stuff like that wore you down, and no amount of sleep seemed to help. He wondered if he had caught Lyme Disease, but he knew he hadn't, because he had none of the symptoms.

On a Saturday morning, having slept in instead of going fishing, he discovered what was wrong.

"Rob," his mother said. "Look at your pants."

He looked down and shook his head. High waters. He'd grown again.

With his back against the door jamb into the kitchen where his parents had measured both boys as they grew, his mother stood on a kitchen stool to make the mark with a square.

He read the tape. Six foot, four inches. He'd caught up to Grandpa Whitmore. "How about that," he said. "No wonder my pitching's been off. I was using up energy growing."

"Grampa's been hoping you'd catch up to him."

He poured a big glass of orange juice and sat at the table looking out across the yard rolling gently into the woods, wondering if explanations were always so easy to come by, or whether some things might never have an explanation. He grinned. That might not be so bad. After all, there were no explanations for fishing, and that was what he liked so much about it. Few things could so consistently take you by surprise.

A car came up the drive, and he walked to the door and stepped out onto the porch as Tom stopped the car and got out. "Ready for your easy throwing day?"

"Yup." He held up his orange juice. "Gotta eat first. I just got up. I'm cooking up some eggs, want some?"

"Naw. I'm stuffed. Mom did waffles this morning and I always eat too many."

They walked into the kitchen. "Want some coffee?"

"Sure, I could go a cup of coffee."

He poured the coffee and set it on the table, watching Tom

put two scoops of sugar in before adding milk. "You got any idea," Tom said, "what you've been doing wrong?"

"I just found out this morning. I've been growing again."

"You're kidding me!"

"Six-four."

"Damn, Robbo! That's a whole foot since September! Is that possible?"

"Must be. I did it."

"You think you're through?"

"I'm the same height as my grandfather now, so probably. At least I don't think I'll grow as fast."

"How do you feel?"

"Tired, but not as tired as I felt the past two weeks. In fact I feel like I've got my energy back."

He heard the phone ring and then his mother called: "Rob, it's for you."

"Okay," he called and then turned to Tom. "Be back in a second," he said, wondering who could be calling. The only person who ever called him was sitting in the kitchen. He walked into the den and picked up the phone.

"Hello?"

"Hi, it's me. The shrew."

He could hear the laughter in her voice. "Mal?"

"When did you send me the book?"

"Three, four weeks ago, at least."

"Well, I just got it in the mail today." There was a silence. "We did that play here last fall," she said. "I played Kate."

He laughed.

"Why is that funny?"

"The coincidence, that's all."

"I thought you must have known."

"I didn't."

"Then why did you send me the book?"

"Because of your letter."

"You sure don't beat around the bush, do you?"

"If you'd told me about your boyfriend in person, I wouldn't have been so angry."

"I kept meaning to tell you. And then I couldn't understand why I didn't, and until I opened this package, I still didn't understand. But now I do."

He didn't know what to say, so he said nothing.

"Rob, this is really hard over the phone. What I'm trying to say is that as of this minute I don't have a boyfriend. He doesn't know that yet, but he will."

And suddenly he felt sad for the other guy, as he remembered what he'd gone through. It wasn't something he'd wish on anyone. "Is this possible?" he asked.

"Yes," she said. "In fact, since that day on the beach, I think it was inevitable."

"I thought so too," he said.

"How's the pitching?" she asked.

"I've been off a little, but I just found out why, at least part of why. I mean, I've been pretty down since I got your last letter, and then I just discovered I grew another inch. I couldn't figure out why I was so tired."

"What does that make you? Six-four?"

"Same as my Grandfather Whitmore."

"That is really strange, Rob. Ever since I was a little girl I wanted to date a guy who was six-four."

"And I always wanted to date you. Do you think we can we pick up where we left off?"

"Are you sure you want to, I mean, me being such a shrew and all?"

"I'll take my chances."

"I'm coming home next weekend, can you meet me at the ferry? I'll be on the ten o'clock. I'm getting a ride with a friend who lives in Falmouth."

"Mal, I'd meet you anywhere, any time, any place."

"Yeah," she said, "me too, but I didn't know that till I got the book."

"I was afraid I'd blown it," he said.

"I really missed you," she said.

"I missed you too, Mal."

Walking on air. Absolutely walking on air, Rob drifted back into the kitchen, smiling the way you smile when hope becomes reality.

"Whoa," Tom said. "Now what?"

"I'm back with Mallory," he said.

"Okay, you're through growing, your love life is straightened out, now maybe we can get back to pitching."

On Tuesday he threw another perfect game. This time there

was only one scout, sitting between his Dad and Hal.

On Saturday, on a warm morning with the fog burning off in a sun yellow haze, he met Mal at the ferry in Vineyard Haven. It was a much warmer greeting than Rob was used to, particularly in public, but it was spontaneous, and not the least bit forced.

All the way out to the house they talked nonstop, the conversation never flagging. They chattered their way right into the house and out to the kitchen where Hal was waiting for them.

"I just got off the phone with your Dad," Hal said.

Rob looked at him carefully, trying to figure out what they had talked about, and guessing it must have had something to do with the house. "Is everything all right with the house?"

"Of course. It had nothing to do with that. What it has to do with is baseball. The short of it, Rob, is that the Mets think you can be a major league pitcher. They'd like you to pitch at Pittsfield this summer. It'll mean signing a contract, and you'll have to negotiate that, but it's not a lot of money at this level."

It was a truly astonishing piece of news. "The Mets?"

Hal grinned. "You may have noticed a guy sitting with me and your dad at the last game. He's one of the top scouts."

"But I haven't hardly pitched!"

"And usually that would be a disadvantage. But in this case it also means you haven't overworked your arm and you haven't spent a lot of time trying pitches that might have caused an injury that just hasn't showed up. And they get to control how you develop."

Rob sat down at the table. "I don't know what to say?"

"Do you want to try it?"

"Sure. Of course."

"You sound a little hesitant," Hal said.

"I've hardly ever been off Island." He looked quickly at Mallory. "And I'd be gone all summer ..."

"We'd come to every game," Hal said. "I go to better than half of them anyway."

"This is *so* exciting," Mallory said.

Rob felt like he'd had too much coffee or maybe too much sugar. "You talked to Dad?"

"Well, I thought I'd better do that first."

Rob smiled. "Good call," he said. "Dad hates to be out of the loop." He stood up and walked across the room to look out the wide windows and off over the tops of the trees at the water sparkling in the distance. "What if it doesn't work out?"

"What do *you* think?" Hal asked. "You up to the challenge?"

Rob nodded and then grinned. "Sure."

"I thought maybe," Hal said. "So did the scout."

Rob grinned. "My head is kind of turning circles here. I feel like I'm standing on the edge of the world."

"Can he really do it?" Mallory asked. "Can he actually pitch in the major leagues?"

Hal grinned. "All Rob has to do is stay healthy, work hard, and learn the game at each level. I'm gonna guess he'll play

Double-A next year and then he'll move pretty quickly to Triple-A. But it may take longer. You need to develop, and your body needs to grow into what you're planning to do with it. Don't for a second think this is in the bag. Very few players make it to the majors. If you wanted to pick an example of a player to model yourself after it would be Roger Clemens. He works year-round and he stays focused."

Mallory looked worried. "What about school?"

"You can easily do a semester a year," Hal said, "before you hit Triple A. After that it's a full time job."

"Twenty-two," Rob said. "I can be there by then."

"How would you feel if you got traded? It happens a lot with young prospects, you know," Hal said.

Rob shrugged. "It's part of the game."

"It is." Hal nodded.

"But I didn't think the Mets were as dumb as the Red Sox."

Hal laughed. "It's part of the game."

Rob reached into his pocket, pulled out the round, sea polished piece of quartz, and held it in the palm of his hand. "It's so amazing," he said, "to think that this can happen because of something so simple as breakin' stones."

Mallory grinned. "... this will be a summer like none that has ever been," she said.

Robert Holland

Robert Holland has a B.A. in history from the University of Connecticut and an M.A. in English from Trinity College. He studied writing under Rex Warner at UConn and under Stephen Minot at Trinity.

He has worked as a journalist, a professor, a stock broker, an editor, and from time to time anything he could make a buck at. He hunts, he is a fly fisherman, a wood-carver, a cabinet maker, and he plays both classical and folk guitar.

While he was never a great athlete, he played with enthusiasm and to some extent overcame his lack of natural ability by teaching himself how to play and then practicing.

Sometime during college he decided he wanted to be a writer and has worked at it ever since, diverting the energy he once poured into sports to becoming not only a writer, but a writer who understands the importance of craft. Like all writers he reads constantly, not only because, as Ernest Hemingway once said, "you have to know who to beat," but because it is the only way to gather the information which every writer must have in his head, and because it is a way to learn how other writers have developed the narrative techniques which make stories readable, entertaining, and meaningful.

He lives in Woodstock, Connecticut, with his wife, Leslie, his daughter Morgan, his son Gardiner, and varying numbers of Labrador retrievers, cats, and chickens.